Shaking The Apple Trees

Copyright © 2004 Janice Monk Glass
All rights reserved.
ISBN: 1-59457-919-9

To order additional copies, please contact us.
BookSurge, LLC
www.booksurge.com
1-866-308-6235
orders@booksurge.com

JANICE
MONK GLASS

SHAKING THE APPLE TREES

THE STORIES OF HENRY JESSE HATTON

2004

Shaking The Apple Trees

To The Old Ones Who Have Passed Through My Life With Their Stories, And To The Young Ones Who Are Making Stories Of Their Own.

CHAPTER 1
A Turn in the Road

Summer 1970

This is a story about the old Benson Community in southeast Arkansas, and you're probably wondering who I am. Well, my name is Henry Jesse Hatton, and my wife is Sarah Jane. Early in our marriage we adopted a newborn boy and named him for Cousin Jake's Pa, Luther Benson. Soon after, we had Cassandra. Then the twins, Charlotte and Victoria came along. A few years later we were surprised by our caboose, Samuel.

Sarah and I came from southwest Missouri where there are cold, snowy mountains and icy roads in winter. We were on our honeymoon in Hot Springs when we decided to drive to Murfreesboro and look for diamonds. Somewhere along the way we made an extra turn in the road. We ended up in front of Miss Annie Bea Teal's Feed & Hardware Store at just about lunch time on Saturday, July the 4th, 1970.

Miss Annie Bea's store has been the unofficial town meeting place ever since anyone can remember. On that day they were having four different celebrations. When we stepped through that door to ask for directions someone put paper plates and plastic forks in our hands and told us to help ourselves.

Jacob Benson and Sallie Mae Nations were being honored with a shower for their wedding to take place the following Saturday. On that same day Jim Bob Jenkins and his wife, Mandy, were celebrating their first wedding anniversary and the birth of their son, James Junior.

It was also the Fourth of July and Miss Annie's warehouse and loading dock were decorated with red, white and blue crepe paper streamers, big colorful stars and bright paper chains. They were hung there the day before by the school young'uns. Tables were set with punch, nuts, cakes and cookies. Other tables had more substantial fixings such as fried chicken, baked beans and tater salad.

Quilts were spread over hay bales, and folks were sitting on hay and sacks of feed, eating, and drinking punch, iced tea and R Cee Colers. There was always a crowd around that punch bowl.

By then Sarah and I were having so much fun we'd plumb forgotten to ask the way to Murfreesboro. We'd been hugged, kissed, hand shook, and patted on the back by so many fine folks that we felt right at home.

Jake's Pa and his Great Uncle Lester brought their fiddles and a mandolin. Three more folks, including me, just happened to have a guitar, a banjo and a bass fiddle out in our pickups. We used the edge of that loading dock for a stage, and it wasn't long before the folks who were drinking that punch were dancing right lively on the parking lot. At sunset we (who could still walk) went to the new community park behind the post office. They'd built an outdoor stage and we could hear the high school band playing *"Under the Double Eagle."* (Mr. Wagner surely did himself proud when he wrote that tune.)

There were more young'uns that Sarah and I thought were possible for one little county. I mentioned that the Lord said, "Go forth and be fruitful."

She retorted, "Yes, but somebody forgot to quit shaking them apple trees."

Then two of the frisky young'uns commenced to run around and toss firecrackers under the old folks' chairs. The sheriff's deputy shooed them away, but they'd come right back. Finally Jake Benson walked over to the two boys, snatched them up and put one under each arm. He dropped them into the back of his truck, growled a few words like "sit and stay" and scowled at them. They sat and stayed.

"My little brothers, Randy and Robbie," Jake grinned. "They ain't scared of Ma and Pa, but I got my bluff in on them early, soon after they were born. They know better than to mess with me." The Bensons and Hattons were friends from the beginning. As it turned out, Sallie and Sarah were second cousins. They hadn't seen each other since they were little girls at a family reunion. They had a lot of catching up to do cause all of their folks from Oklahoma were there for the showering.

Later that night Jake's Pa, Luther Benson, wouldn't hear of Sarah and me going to a motel. He boomed, "Why, we've got all kinds of room out there on the farm. You're welcome to stay as long as you like. You're going to stay for the wedding I know. I heard Sallie Mae ask Sarah to be her maid of honor."

They gave us the boys' room. The two young'uns were tickled pink to sleep in the hayloft. "If I hear any mischief from the barn out of you two," Jake told them, "you won't be eating breakfast in the morning, and I know how much you two like your biscuits and sausage gravy." At night we heard nary a peep from the twin boys the whole time we stayed.

Mrs. Benson was pregnant with Becky Sue. Sallie and Sarah helped her gather vegetables. They canned jars of tomatoes, purple hull peas, and soup. Then they chopped cabbages and packed them with brine into stoneware crocks for sauerkraut. Later they sliced cucumbers and made sweet pickles.

Jake and I helped the girls plant a fall turnip patch. We played and threw dirt clods at each other. We had a big time. Jake's folks watched us and laughed, "It's nice to have lots of young folks around." Then Jake's Ma sent us down to the pump to wash away the dirt before she'd let us come to supper.

That night Sarah and I watched the moon from the bedroom window. "I've never been so tired in my life," she whispered, "or so happy. I love this farming land and these people." She leaned her head on my shoulder. "Jake and Sallie Mae will raise their young'uns on this flat land. They'll never have to fret about them falling off a mountainside like my little brother did. I wish we didn't have to leave."

I agreed with her. For a week Jake, his Pa, Randy, Robbie and I had split and stacked firewood, repaired fences, cleaned barns and built a new smokehouse for hog killing time in November. I'd never had a pa to teach me these skills; he'd left us when I was three. My mama did the best she could, but she was away from home much of the time trying to make us a living. Now I enjoyed learning as I worked with the Bensons.

By the time Great Grandpa Benson's clock struck midnight that night, Sarah and I knew what we wanted to ask Luther the next day. But we didn't have to ask.

After breakfast Luther and Jake said they had something they wanted to show us. We all piled into Jake's noisy, old pickup and bounced down a rutted dirt road to neglected homesteads. We walked over the brushy, overgrown fields and down to the river. There would be months of back breaking clearing before this land produced crops again.

This was Jake's Grandpa's place. He didn't want to be a farmer; he was off playing music somewhere. Jake looked with love across the fields. "Grandpa wants to sell it; I want to buy it, but there's way too much land for one man to farm by himself. If I could buy it reasonable enough, I could sell half of it and we'd both still have plenty of farming land." Then he grinned, "Sure would be a good place to plant those apple trees y'all were talking about."

I looked towards the river and the fertile plains. There were barns, chicken coops and two weathered old plantation houses with enough rooms to raise all the little apples we wanted.

Jake studied me, "The houses were built by my great grandpa and his bachelor son. Both houses are furnished. My Grandpa inherited them when his Pa and brother passed away. Sallie's Cousin Jim Bob and his wife, Mandy Lee, have the adjoining land there to the east. If that field was cleared you could see their house over on the county road."

Sarah had that dreamy look in her eyes; the one she got in the jewelry store when she saw those big diamonds and all we could afford was a small gold wedding band. I promised her one day she'd have a diamond, even bigger. "It doesn't matter," she'd whispered then. "You and I are all that matters now."

But this time it did matter. I could see the longing in her misty eyes as she gazed across that land and looked back at the houses. We ached for this land. We belonged here. Our fruit and our faith would grow deep in and on this soil. I didn't know how we would do it. Sarah and I didn't have two quarters to rub together, but I took her hand and told Jake and his Pa, "Sarah and I will buy this half we're standing on here." And that's how a turn in the road one day brought us from Missouri to Arkansas to the land and the people we love.

CHAPTER 2
Loving the Land

Autumn 1970

J ake's Grandpa sold us the land for a hundred dollars down, a handshake apiece and our promises to pay him as we could.

Jim Bob and Mandy Lee helped us paint and clean our houses. The girls made curtains and dusted furniture. They scrubbed cast iron kitchen stoves, pine floors, walls and cabinets. Then they put all the wedding gifts in their places. Jake's Ma made wedding ring quilts and put one on each of our beds. Twenty five years later they're still there.

The whole community turned out for the houses warming. When the men saw the work needed on the neglected farm buildings, they were there every Saturday morning until the barns, coops and fences were as good as new. Our neighbors even built a smokehouse for us.

Mandy Lee gave Sallie and Sarah some laying hens to go in their chicken yards. Jim Bob's pa, Chester Jenkins, gave each girl six more hens and brought us a little Jersey cow ready to freshen. Explained he was already milking two cows and his arthritis wouldn't let him milk a third one everyday. Over the years the cow, Daisy, and her offspring gave enough milk for both families. Uncle Chester never asked for them back, nor would he take any money for them.

Jake's Pa bought himself a tractor, so he brought us his team of strong work mules, Molly and Bullet. It didn't take long for Sarah and Sallie to make pets of the lovable animals. A few years later we gave Molly to Uncle Chester. They were both getting old and slow, and worked together just fine.

Jim Bob loaned Sarah and me his flatbed trailer, and we went to Missouri to get our belongings. Neither of us had much; a few clothes, my grandpa's antique typewriter and Sarah's treasured books. She brought her little spinet piano and her grand mother's iron bedstead and marble washstand for our room. Someone tossed on a feather bed. We were pleased with that feather bed at the time.

Her mama gave us a dozen mixed pullets and two roosters. We put them in crates tied to the trailer. Then her Uncle Billy came by with his wedding gift for us, a pair of young Nubian kids. He told us they'd eat down the unwanted brush on the new place. But he didn't tell us they'd also eat our newly planted fruit orchards, our fall vegetable gardens, the chickens' feed and Jake's best overalls off the line.

Uncle Simon and Aunt Isabelle gave us a pair of geese and promised they'd keep snakes away. I was proud of the geese as I don't hold with any snakes. Aunt Isabelle sent along an apple pie, a new handmade quilt, embroidered dish towels, and three quacking white ducks.

We tied the goats away from the piano to they couldn't eat the legs off it, but we plumb forgot about the feather bed. As we drove down Highway 7 in the Ozark Mountains, we looked back and saw flashing blue lights through swirling white feathers. The goats had eaten the ticking off that feather bed. It's a good thing the state trooper was a country boy. Claimed he'd write me a ticket for littering, but he felt sorry for us because we'd lost our soft, warm feather bed. Besides, he was laughing so hard he couldn't write anyway.

A few hours later we pulled into the yard of our new home. By then the goats had gnawed through the top of the poultry crates. When we stopped, the chickens, ducks and geese came out of the cages and commenced to scattering. Jake grabbed his fish dipping net and scooped up chickens. We put them into the pen. Bantams and guineas that flew into the trees came down in a day or two when they got hungry. The ducks headed toward the lake, and the geese went with them. They never came back to the house.

Sarah gave Sallie half of the mixed pullets and one of the young roosters. Sallie named the rooster "Henry" after me. As the years passed, so did a lot of "Henrys."

Later Uncle Billy asked how the goats were. We told him they were just fine. At dinner time on Thanksgiving and Christmas they were just fine, too,—- hot off that barbeque grill.

The four of us walked together across the September fields. We knew we were truly blessed with everything we needed. We had land, homes and friends we knew we could always depend on. All we needed now were some young'uns, a dog or two, and a crop to sell. We were working on all of them.

Then Hiram Potter from across the creek came over and gave us two lanky red-tick pups. It was almost hunting season and Hiram told us, "They're old enough to hunt this year, and ever'body needs 'em a good hunting dawg."

Next Sallie and Sarah gave Jake and me some happy news. Now all we needed was a crop.

CHAPTER 3
Little Ben

Winter 1971

Sarah Jane's sister, Emily Ann, ran away from home when she was seventeen. She'd always wanted to be a movie star. After Emily got to California she called herself "Amelia" and got small parts in movies nobody ever heard about.

It was a cold, hard winter in Missouri that January of 1971. Sarah's mama, Miss Elizabeth, had felt poorly since Thanksgiving with a cold she couldn't get over. Sarah and her mama wrote long, newsy letters back and forth every week. We commenced to worry when we hadn't heard from her in two weeks. Then young Deputy Johnson came to our door with bad news.

Emily-Amelia had come home from California a week earlier and found Miss Elizabeth alone in the house and bad sick. She took her to the hospital. Sarah's mama had passed away with pneumonia in a Missouri hospital.

Jake's pa, Luther, insisted we take his new four wheel drive truck. Roads in Missouri were icy and we might need it. Sarah was six months pregnant and Luther's new truck had a camper, and the seats were more comfortable for her.

Miss Elizabeth's passing presented a real problem to Emily. She was in the family way and had come home to have the baby. She had no use for a young'un and had planned on leaving it with her mama to find a home for it while she resumed her movie career in California. The baby's papa was long gone. He was a married man and wanted nothing to do with Emily or his young'un.

Emily went into labor two days after the funeral. Three days later, she placed the little boy child into the arms of Uncle Simon who was a preacher, and asked Simon to find a home for him. She declared that she'd made a new life and would never come back to Missouri. As far as she was concerned we could consider her dead, too

Sarah and I lay awake in her mama's mountain home long into the night after Emily left for California. I wondered how two girls who were sisters could be so different. My Sarah was kind and caring; Emily was cold and unfeeling. And we talked about the little dark eyed, tow headed young'un who was our nephew. He looked enough like Sarah to be her own child.

"How can we let strangers have him?" she cried. "I already love him like he's my own child." She turned to me with tears in her eyes, "Do you think they'll teach him right and take him to church and raise him to be a good man?"

Dawn had streaked the sky, and we'd made our decision. Poor as church mice, we could hardly take care of ourselves. We didn't know a thing about babies except that they were to be loved. How in the world were we going to care for two at once? We knelt beside the bed and asked our Lord to show us the way. Then we called Jake and Sallie for their blessings and support.

An hour later Sarah and I went to see Uncle Simon. Aunt Isabelle met us at the door with a smile on her face and the baby in her arms. She whispered, "He's a precious child; we prayed you'd come for him"

We'd planned to name our first son after Jake's pa, Luther Benson. When we drove into our yard that night Luther Benson Hatton was sleeping peacefully in his loving mama's arms.

CHAPTER 4
Ol' Red Dog
Autumn 1972

Hiram Potter sued the state when their dump truck ran over his ol' red tick hound dog.. That ol' red hound dog wasn't ever worth anything. He just stayed under the front porch and slept all day. Most he ever did was gather ticks and fleas, scatter dog hair, draw flies, and steal eggs from the hen house.. Sometimes, if a stranger went by, he'd poke out his head and bellow a time or two, but he wasn't bad, just loud.

The day that Horace Smith's lady dog came to visit, the lazy ol' scoot took himself out to the driveway to greet her. Just about that time Homer Lee Chism decided to turn around that big orange dump truck in Hiram's driveway. That day the flea bitten ol' red dog become the most valuable coon hound in three states. The worth Hiram put on him was more than all he owned, with the house, his hidden whiskey still and his shotgun thrown in.

After Hiram got his cash—he wouldn't take any check; said he didn't hold with no banks—somebody left a bony, yellow and white speckled pup right in front of his house. Now Hiram is trying to teach the pup to sleep in the driveway, but Hiram's wife, Mildred, says if he sucks any more hen eggs, she ain't waiting for another dump truck.

CHAPTER 5
She Walked Like a Duck

Winter 1973

Deputy Potter's Mama, Miss Viola, was one of those ladies who walked like a duck. You know the ones I mean; the kind that's all bosoms up front and all fannies out back, and just can't help walking like a duck.

Jake couldn't keep from grinning every time he saw her. He couldn't help himself. No amount of pointy jabs from Sallie Mae's sharp elbow could completely wipe that grin off his face.

Miss Viola played the pump organ at church every Sunday. She played by ear and she knew every song in the hymn book. When folks started singing, she felt the glory of The Lord and began stomping those organ pedals.

Jake and I held our breaths and prayed the rocking piano bench wouldn't collapse. Every once in awhile we took it home with us and hammered in more nails and dabbed on lots of wood glue for reinforcement.

It was our third year on the farm. Jake and I had been busy clearing fields and planting a peach orchard all winter. We didn't notice Miss Viola had gained a few more pounds over the holidays, and we plumb forgot about the celebration until it was too late to check the piano bench.

The second Sunday of every February we celebrate President Lincoln's and President Washington's birthdays. It's a tradition at our church to brighten up dreary Februarys. Everybody comes home, and we have singing all day, visiting and potluck in the fellowship hall. That year the Sunday school young'uns painted big pictures of the presidents and stood them in front of the pulpit. They made red, white, and blue paper chains to drape over the pews. Big, silver stars left from Christmas hung in all the windows. It looked real patriotic.

Ol' Grandpa Cummings, who founded the church sixty years ago, always came back to deliver the sermon. It was the same message year after year about Washington crossing the Delaware and being honest by not telling lies. He told how Lincoln read his Bible by firelight and walked miles in the snow to return a book he'd borrowed, and on and on. We all knew it by heart.

So did Miss Viola. She sat with feet on the pedals and hands raised above the keys. When Brother Cummings hollered "Amen," her feet stomped those pedals and her fingers whipped the keys in her zealous rendition of "Onward Christian Soldiers."

Jake nudged me with his elbow and nodded towards the piano bench. It swayed and wobbled. One of the legs was moving. Jake and I started towards Miss Viola, but we didn't get there in time.

The congregation was halfway through the second verse. Everyone was standing. They were clapping their hands, stomping their feet and singing at the tops of their voices when that leg popped off and flipped Miss Viola into the front pew of the congregation. Everyone hushed.

She grabbed that leg, rose to her feet and commenced to march down the aisle singing "Onward Christian Soldiers." She waved that bench leg over her head like a sword. When she marched for The Lord, she didn't walk like a duck anymore. Soon we were all marching behind her and singing. We marched out the front door and around the church house still singing.

Jake built Miss Viola a sturdy new bench. He wouldn't let me help him; claimed it was something he had to do. Miss Viola's been gone a long time, but she used the new bench for years before she passed on. It never wobbled.

Jake keeps the broken bench leg hanging on a wall in his workshop. He says it's his reminder that it isn't how a person looks, but what's in their heart that makes them special.

CHAPTER 6
"Serpent, Be Gone!"

Spring 1974

Jake could fuss worse than anybody in Little River County. He kept the hair blistered off the hindquarters of Ol' Bullet, just for stepping on a row. Folks would say—behind his back, of course,—that Jake could have a barbeque and never light a fire.

The preacher had heard all the stories about him, but Cousin Jake never fussed in front of the preacher. He sat in church wearing the sweet face of an angel, with his hands folded in the lap of his clean overalls and listen with rapture to Brother Cummings preaching.

Once a month we had a singing and dinner on the ground after the preaching. The ladies brought baskets filled with home cooking and put them on red checked oil cloths spread on long, weathered tables under big, shady oak trees. Families sat on the ground on quilts and blankets. Everyone shared the repast after Brother Cummings said the blessing.

Brother Cummings could get a little long winded at times, while the cornbread got cold, and the bacon grease settled on the bowls of black eyed peas. And that fried chicken—all that tasty fried chicken—was just setting there waiting for my mouth.

Sallie made the best fried chicken in the county, and Jake was sitting there with his head bowed and rolling his eyes over that platter of chicken. Then he spotted something else: a big bad copperhead snake easing up among all of us with our heads bowed in prayer.

Jake touched Sallie Mae's arm, but she scrunched her eyes tighter and shook her head at him. Cousin Jake didn't know whether to bring down the wrath of God, Brother Cummings and Sallie Mae, and jump up and warn everyone about the reptile, who was moving awfully close, or behave himself and take a chance on somebody getting snake bit.

Then Jake got an idea. He jumped up shouting and grabbed an old grubbing hoe left there from the cemetery cleaning. He yelled, "Serpent, be gone! Be gone, I say from these brethren." He ran around and whacked the old copperhead right smart and threw him back into the woods. Then he shouted, "The serpent is gone, Lord; the serpent is gone!"

Everybody thought Jake was saved. They raised their heads, opened their eyes, and jumped up shouting, "Amen! Amen!" They shook his hand and patted him on the back while the food got colder.

Now Jake does his fussing on the far field out of hearing of Sallie Mae and the neighbors. Jake thinks nobody ever knew what really happened. Nobody does, except me. I had my eye on the platter of fried chicken and that snake, too. But I don't hold with any snakes; I ain't a hero. Besides, that snake wouldn't have had a chance with those Methodists when Brother Cummings yelled, "AMEN, NOW LET'S EAT!"

CHAPTER 7
Judgment Day

Summer 1975

"There ain't no way you're going to do it!" Sallie Mae shouted.

"I will if I want to, and nothing you can say will stop me," Jake snorted.

Sarah Jane and I were easing out the back door. When Jake and Sallie argue things have a way of flying at their house; and it ain't always just words.

Sallie stood with hands on her hips and fire in her eyes. "I ain't going to let you!"

Jake was nervous. He knew that look, but he wouldn't back down. "I gave my word that I'd do it, and a man doesn't go back on his word."

"What are the preacher and everybody going to say 'bout you and Jim Bob judging a wet tee shirt contest?" Sallie was still shouting.

"Ain't any of anybody's business except mine and Jim Bob's, and we've made up our minds to be the judges." Jake slammed out the front door and headed for Jim Bob's place.

There was a week of cold war and cold sandwiches at both houses. On the night of the contest Jake got into his truck and went to pick up Jim Bob.

When they left, Sallie and Mandy got into Mandy's car and sped away.

I watched out the window. "Their two wives are up to something." I turned to Sarah, "Do you know what it is?"

"You'll find out soon enough," she laughed. "I promised not to tell anyone, not even you, but get your cap and truck keys. We ain't missing this for anything!"

At the contest the judges were introduced to the audience and were seated on the front row. House lights went off and the stage lights came on. The red velvet curtains slowly parted.

All the contestants in their wet tee shirts and tight jeans wiggled onto the stage. Jake and Jim Bob took one look and gasped.

Jim Bob jumped up yelling, "Mandy! What in thunder's name do you think you and Sallie are doing up there? Y'all get down from there right now!"

For once, Jake was speechless. His eyes were bugged on Sallie Mae as she sashayed across the stage. He looked like he'd seen a ghost. Real awkward he stumbled to his feet. "How could you do this to me," he croaked. "Everyone is looking at you."

"Mandy and I decided if you can't beat them, then join them. If you can judge the contest, then we can enter it." She stuck out her wet chest and tossed her long, dark hair over her shoulders.

The audience howled, stomped and applauded. Needless to say, Jake and Jim Bob were excused as judges by the contest officials because their wives were contestants.

Jake and Jim Bob haven't offered to judge anymore wet tee shirt contests, and their wives haven't entered any more. But Sallie Mae and Mandy Lee are right proud of those first and second place trophies setting on shelves in their closets.

CHAPTER 8
Critter

Spring 1976

Jake and I were pulling the boat to Millwood Lake to fish when we saw Widow Johnson standing by her car at the side of the road. We stopped to see if she needed help.

She pointed across the ditch. There was a baby alligator sunning himself on the bank below us. He was about a foot and a half long.

"I'd sure like to have him as a pet for my grand young'uns," she appealed to us.

Jake told her, "Miss Johnson, your grandbabies don't need that thing. It would bite off all their fingers."

"Oh no," she remarked, "I'd put him in one of those big, glass fish tanks so they could look at him. He's just a baby."

Jake studied on what she'd said.. Then he hooked his thumbs in his overalls, leaned over and looked her in the eye. "Miss Johnson, he may be just a baby, but catching that little critter would take two brave, strong men with lots of guts. Jesse and I ain't them."

CHAPTER 9
The Biggest Fish
Spring 1977

Jim Bob Jenkins lived to fish. When he heard of a bass tournament over in East Texas one Saturday he decided to enter it. His long time fishing buddy, Horace Smith, told him he'd heard all the prizes were running upwards to five thousand dollars. They had as good a chance of winning as anybody. Maybe better.

A couple of weeks earlier Jim Bob had caught two big striped basses on Lake Greeson. He took them home and tossed them into the freezer thinking he'd have them mounted. Now one of these big basses might be his ace-in-the-fishing-hole if he didn't catch something bigger on Saturday. He'd just take one along, thaw him out, weigh him in and go home a rich man. Horace would never tell.

Mandy and Faye were always complaining because they fished so much while the crops went to weeds. If they won any money, they'd give some of it to the church to make their wives happy.

On the day of the tournament Jim Bob and Horace hitched up the boat trailer and threw in some extra things they might need. They got to the lake just in time to pay their entry fee and start out with the others.

Horace trolled while Jim Bob followed the boats to see what the others did since neither of them had fished in a tournament nor been on that lake before. The motor died when they'd been on the lake about twenty minutes. While Jim Bob tinkered with the engine, Horace caught some small basses and threw them back. By the time they were running again the others were out of sight. They didn't know which way the other fishermen went so they decided to stay put and cast towards that far bank; it appeared a likely spot.

Jim Bob kept his eye on those black clouds over towards the southwest. He didn't hold with being on the water in a lightning and thunder storm, but Horace was starting to catch some fish and wanted to stay there. By noon they'd caught a few small ones and threw them all back. Jim Bob checked the frozen lunker. He was thawing real nice; they'd probably have to use him.

They each had several sandwiches, big bags of chips, and plastic two liter bottles of R Cee Coler. By the time they'd finished eating the sky was overcast, and Horace had caught a couple of three pound bass.

Jim Bob was really good at finding his way by the slant of the sun, but the sun was gone. They were on an unfamiliar lake, a storm was brewing, and they were as turned around as a northbound goose flying south. Jim Bob eased the boat down a brushy channel, thinking it was a shortcut back to the boat ramp.

Weigh in time came around. Jim Bob and Horace hadn't come in. Soon everyone was weighed, and folks commenced to fret about them. Worried fishermen went looking for them. An hour later they found them hanging onto their boat in a stumpy channel. The biggest wasp nest they'd ever seen was in a bush next to them. Appeared the ol' waterlogged, bug bitten boys got lost and jumped out of the boat when they hit that wasp nest.

To make a long story short, the tournament officials voted to award the first place prize money to them because of that big ol' fish they had in their live-well. By then the fish was glassy eyed, but hey, it was only fair. After all, it was the biggest fish they'd weighed all day.

The next morning Jim Bob and Horace gave all their winnings to the preacher. Their wives and Brother Cummings looked as pleased as punch.

Jim Bob and Horace figured that God put the wasp nest there for a reason, and who were they to question Him. Besides, the church house needed painting, new boards for the front porch and new shingles. If there was any money left, they'd give it to the Ladies' Sunday School Class for their steeple bell fund.

They may even take off a weekend or two from fishing to help with all the work; but not next Saturday. There's a tournament at Millwood Lake they'd better not miss because the young'uns need a new Sunday school room. And Jim Bob still has one big ol' fish left in his freezer.

CHAPTER 10
The Worst Rat

Spring 1978

Nobody knew anything about the checkbook that was missing. I'd put it back on the dresser after I bought the new tires last week. Sarah said she saw it last when she wrote a check to Hiram for the firewood he'd brought. The young'uns didn't write checks, so where could it have gone?

Then Sarah began to notice other things missing. Her thimble was gone from the table beside the quilt she was making. "Why would anyone take a thimble?" she had asked. Then the small, golden broach I'd given her for our fifth wedding anniversary disappeared from her jewelry box. She cried for hours.

Coins began to leave from the dish on the dresser. My prized pocket knife Papa Luther gave me for Christmas the year before he died was gone. I felt like crying, too. Then things really got serious. Sarah cut her finger just below her wedding ring. When her finger began to swell she removed the ring and placed it in her jewelry box before we went to bed. The next morning the ring was gone. Enough was enough.

I gathered all the young'uns and sat them down for a discussion. I told them that somebody was taking things, and that somebody was right here in this house. I watched their mama put that ring in the jewelry box last night, and nobody else was in the house but us. They all shook their little heads. Their innocent eyes filled with tears. How could I think my babies would steal? I looked at all their sweet little faces and felt like a rat.

But each night something else disappeared: more coins, another ring, a shiny button from Sarah's blouse. Finally I decided to lie awake with a flashlight in my hand to catch the culprit. No one came that night, but nothing was missing either. In the back of my mind I still wondered if it was a young'un. I felt like a rat to even think it.

The next night I heard a faint scratching sound from the fireplace in our room. I watched as a large pack rat crept across the floor, climbed up the covers at the foot of our bed and jumped to the dresser. She went straight to Sarah's jewelry box and nosed open the lid.

I don't hold with any rats. In my opinion, rats are one step below snakes on my list of horrors. I jumped out of bed yelling and flung a boot at her. She fled up the chimney with an earring in her mouth. Sarah woke from a sound sleep to find me with my head up the chimney cussing a rat.

The next morning I carefully removed some of the bricks in the fireplace. Before I began, I told Sarah and the young'uns to stand out of my way. If that rat came out of the chimney I didn't want to hurt someone. We found all our missing possessions in the pack rat's nest. She'd shredded the checkbook and used it and quilt batting to make a soft place for her babies. They weren't born yet, and I was glad. Don't know what I would have done; Sarah and the young'uns would have insisted on making pets of them.

Everything is back in its place. The pregnant rat moved elsewhere, and the young'uns have forgiven me for thinking they could steal. When I think about the tears I caused, I still think the worst rat was this two legged one.

CHAPTER 11
My Son

Summer 1978

Ever since the morning Sarah and I took Baby Ben from Uncle Simon's house, we'd lived with the fear that one day Emily-Amelia would change her mind and come looking for him. Nobody knew where he'd gone except Uncle Simon and Aunt Isabelle who were elderly at the time. They'd both gone to be with Jesus and nobody knew he wasn't our natural son except Sallie, Jake and his parents.

Ben was born a small baby of five pounds. Winter was cold and we kept him hidden at home. We didn't want anyone to know we had him until we could decide how to make him legally ours. We never got around to it.

Cassie was born in April. She was a hefty nine pounds. We lay her in the crib with three month old Ben who'd just reached nine pounds. The tow headed, dark eyed babies looked like twins. Sarah and I thought of the deception at the same time. We prayed The Lord could forgive our lie, but we knew what we had to do.

On Sunday morning Sarah and I proudly carried our new twin babies to the altar for christening. Jake and Sallie each held a godchild as they were named Luther Benson and Cassandra Elizabeth. After the church services everyone gathered around to comment on our two precious, healthy babies.

Miss Viola Potter, the community news carrier, looked at Sarah and commented, "Where in the world did you carry both of them babies? You didn't look that large. Why with no more weight that you gained it must have been all babies."

My little Sarah smiled at Miss Potter.

"Yes, and ain't it nice? I don't have any baby fat to lose."

Two weeks later Sarah and I stood with Jake and Sallie when five day old Jacob Adam Benson, Junior, was christened.

Ben and Cassie were seven year olds when Emily-Amelia and her new husband showed up on our doorstep. She demanded to know who'd adopted her child. They'd been to Missouri to find him and nobody knew anything about an adoption at the courthouse. She assumed that Uncle Simon had told us the identity of his new ma and pa.

My guts twisted into a knot. Through a sickening haze of fear I heard Sarah's controlled half lie, "No, we left for Arkansas after he was born, and Uncle Simon never told us when he was adopted. Thought about taking him ourselves, but I was pregnant with twins. We couldn't care for three babies at once."

Sarah paled, and I probably did, too, when Emily looked through the window at the rambunctious young'uns playing dodge-ball outside. "Whose boy is that?" She demanded to know. "Call him inside, I want to get a good look at him." Sarah mentioned to her that Ben was Cassie's twin.

The disheveled young'uns all came inside and were introduced to their aunt and Uncle Ray who appeared bored with the matter. When Emily saw Ben and Cassie she sputtered, "Why, my child would be handsome; those two kids are as plain as chicken tracks. Ain't no mistaking they're brother and sister."

After the young'uns went back outside to play, Sarah took a deep breath and inquired, "Why do you want the child after all this time, Emily?"

"My name's Amelia. Don't ever forget it."

"I asked you, why do you want the child after all this time?"

"His real daddy is a big shot TV star who's worth millions now. I never signed any papers giving the kid away. Rightfully he's still mine. Ray says if we can find the kid we can sue his ol' man for a bundle in past and future child support."

Sarah was horrified. "You wouldn't! What if he denies it?"

"Oh yes, we would! If he denies it I'll just show him all those pictures we took together. He'll either pay child support or blackmail; I don't care which, just so we get our money."

"And then what?" I managed to croak.

"We'll put that kid in a boarding school somewhere and travel to all those places I've always wanted to see."

Visions of Ben imprisoned in a boarding school raced through my mind. The thought of Ben, not being with us to fish, swim, or ride his pony across green fields with his sisters and cousins sickened me. I couldn't imagine not seeing Ben's shy smile and knowing his kindness every day as he lovingly tended to hurt or sick animals. He wanted to be a veterinarian.

I was red-faced angry and ready to explode. Heat burning under my collar was making me angrier. I rose to my feet sputtering, trying to talk.

Sarah was fretting about what I was going to say. She interrupted me with, "Ain't it a shame that Uncle Simon and Aunt Isabelle are both gone? There are no records, so it was a private adoption. They're the only ones who knew who wanted the little feller. Now you'll never know where he is."

Emily-Amelia sat thinking about that and fanning herself with a large, pink feathered fan. Reminded me of those bright pink flamingos we saw at the Little Rock Zoo. I wondered if they killed those pretty birds so people like her could fan themselves. Seemed a shame if they did.

Sarah opened the front door. "I'd ask y'all to stay, but I know you're ready to get out of our Arkansas heat and return to California where it's nice and cool. Sure been good seeing you again, Emily. Have a safe trip home."

Sarah and I were so unnerved we took the rest of the day off. Sarah filled the picnic basket, and we took the young'uns to the lake to swim. Ben leaned against me on the quilt and asked, "Why was Aunt Emily so mean to us, Dad?" I hugged him close to me and answered, "Maybe she's not really mean, Son. She's just different from the folks we know."

Someday, I'll have to tell him the truth. If he wants to, we'll help him find her. I pray he'll understand we kept the truth from him all these years because we love him. Whatever the consequences to Sarah and me later, we'll know we did the best for Ben at the time.

CHAPTER 12
Catfish and Chicken Legs
Spring 1979

Jake and I go fishing every Thursday after we finish the chores. One day we loaded our poles and headed to the lake where we keep a battered old wooden boat.

Sallie sent along her Sunday-go-to-meeting picnic basket with her famous fried chicken in it. Her Cherokee mama made that basket and Sallie was real fond of it.

Jake and I would gnaw on those chicken bones and toss them overboard. Nothing could draw catfish like those chicken bones could. We didn't use any of that fancy fishing gear; just some cane poles, blood bait and pork rinds we'd made after we killed the hogs.

Catfish were fairly jumping on our hooks that day while we sat there and ate that fried chicken. We weren't paying attention that we'd drifted near a willow thicket. Jake had left the lid open on the basket, and we looked just in time to see an arm sized cottonmouth dropping off a tree limb into that basket.

I don't hold with any snakes. Just as I was trying to get the dumb out of my legs and jump out of the boat, Jake reached his hand into the basket. He grabbed that big bad snake where his ears ought to be, smacked his head on the side of the boat and chunked him way out into the lake.

"Are you crazy or something?" I yelled. "Why'd you take a chance like that for? Why didn't you just kick basket and all out of the boat?"

Cousin Jake looked me straight in the eye and said, "I thought of it, but I knew we'd have to face Sallie Mae about her basket. Besides, there's still a chicken leg left, and I wasn't about to let a snake have it!"

I had my eye on that last chicken leg, too. But that's all right; Jake earned it.

CHAPTER 13
The Rain Dance
Summer 1979

It was the hottest and driest summer anyone could remember. Some folks claimed the air was so full of dust they could take a deep breath, roll it around on their tongues and spit mud balls.

Sunday morning, in the church house, Brother Cummings announced that our Native American neighbors were planning a rain dance over at their place. Several tribes would be dancing in their tribal dress. They called it a "Pow Wow." Our congregation was invited to go over and join them to pray for rain.

Jake stood up and protested, "I don't hold with no rain dancing. The Lord will make it rain when it's time. We can do our praying right here."

Then Jim Bob Jenkins stood up and commenced to talk. "I think we should go over there and help them all we can. It don't matter how we talk to God just so He knows we're all in agreement that we need rain." Most folks, including Sallie Mae and me, agreed with Jim Bob.

Cousin Jake was all bent out of shape on the day of the rain dance. He probably wouldn't have gone at all, except he watched Sallie Mae wring the necks on all those fryers the day before, and he knew her basket was plumb full of fried chicken. At dinner time, if he stayed at home, he'd have cold biscuits and gravy left from breakfast, and he didn't hold with any cold food.

I put our wives, kids and picnic baskets in my ol' utility van and drove twenty eight miles across the state line to a park in McCurtain County. Jake sat on the passenger side and sulked all the way. He'd said nary a word all day.

Everyone met in the middle of a big, sunny field that was running alive with those fire ants. The womenfolk visited while they spread the food on tables under a large, airy building they called a pavilion.

The dancers gathered amongst us all. They invited us to dance with them and showed us how to make the steps. Our whole congregation was there, taking the dancing lessons along with a congregation from DeKalb and one from Gillham. Everyone except Cousin Jake, that is. He was rambling around mumbling to himself and looking for a place to sit down.

We all took our places and prepared to start the rain dance. Everyone gathered round to watch us, and it got real quiet. Real soft like, the drums started to beat, the bells began to jingle and the dancers began to dance.

All of a sudden Cousin Jake jumped up and ran amongst the group, dancing first on one leg, then on t'other. He flapped both arms, shook his legs and kept on dancing, whooping all the time. He hollered, jumped high and slapped his legs, all red in the face and teary eyed. What he was doing must have been right because clouds commenced to form over to the southwest.

We all plumb forgot them rain dance steps. We all joined Jake, dancing what he was doing. The higher we whooped, jumped and slapped our legs, the darker the clouds got. The wind blew harder and big raindrops fell. The wives and young'uns ran to the pavilion, but Jake and we kept on dancing. Why, Cousin Jake danced right out of his overalls.

Driving home in the rain that night, we sang gospel songs and smelled sweet rain soaking into the earth. Now Jake's grumbling because it ain't quit raining for nigh onto two weeks. He wants it to stop cause the river's too high and swift and he can't go fishing.

Sallie Mae, who is a Native American herself, says it serves him right for dancing the wrong dance. If he hadn't been all pouty faced that day he would have noticed he was sitting down in a fire ant bed.

CHAPTER 14
Train Ride

Autumn 1980

Jake and I heard about a Confederate railroad with real steam engines in the next county. We decided to take our families for a train ride and a picnic. Now Cousin Jake and I ain't always up to date on the latest events. We'd never heard of any "Civil War Reenactment" so we got the surprise of our lives early one Saturday morning when we drove into the park and glanced over towards the woods.

Camped amongst the trees were blue uniformed Yankees of every size, shape and description. They were shaving, playing radios, cleaning rifles and just sitting around talking. They even had their wives with them. Some of them were cooking breakfast over campfires. It was a siege for sure because tents were everywhere. And may the saints save us! They had a cannon pointed right towards us—and a pile of cannon balls to shoot in it.

Jake slammed on the brakes and rearranged wives, young'uns and picnic baskets back there in the camper. Sallie Mae came out of that camper like a scalded hen. "What's gotten into you now?" she screamed. "Have you completely lost your mind?"

Jake reached for his shotgun and yelled, "Yankees! Look at all of them! Get back in the truck, woman! We've got to warn everybody!" The Yankees all stopped what they were doing and stared at us. Jake glared back at them.

Sallie Mae calmed him some by pointing over towards the depot. The depot platform and the train were plumb running over with Rebels holding rifles. We were well protected. But Jake still didn't hold with any Yankees, so it took some talking to make him put his shotgun back on the gun rack and go on the train ride.

We all got on the train and commenced to enjoy ourselves. The young'uns were hanging out the windows. Sallie and Sarah were taking pictures of the young'uns; two loud, male tourists in colorful flowered Hawaiian shirts; and the Rebel guards talking and laughing together.

The old Civil War steam engines and depot were movie props left behind after the filming was completed years ago. Passenger cars were finished on their outsides but only had wooden benches on their insides. There weren't any window panes and sooty ashes blew on us—just like in the olden days.

The weather was really nice that day. Leaves were changing colors, and busy squirrels were everywhere. On a hillside we saw a deer doe and her half grown young'un. Oh, it was a fine day all right—until the Yankees attacked the train.

When the train stopped, and the shooting started, Sallie and Sarah put the young'uns on the floor.. Jake and I followed the Rebs out the door. On the way we both grabbed up big pieces of firewood off the engine and waded into the Yankees.

"Hey, Man, don't take it so seriously," one of the Yanks yelled. "We're just play acting."

"I ain't play acting," Jake hollered back, still swinging firewood. "My wife and young'uns are on that train you're shooting at."

I never saw or heard so much smoke, shooting and shouting in my life, but it didn't take long, with Jake and me helping, to send most of them back into the woods and capture the rest of them. We put the Yank prisoners into the open car that was directly behind the engine. They were well guarded by Rebs, and we finished the trip to the turn around.

The turn around is a big turntable in the ground near the end of the tracks. The engine is unhooked from the cars and driven onto that turn around. The passengers get off the train, grab a hold on a long pole and help push the engine around.

While we were turning the engine, Jake was checking out the first car: you know, the one filled with Yankees and Rebel guards. He wondered what the lever on the hitch did so he gave it a good, firm shove, but nothing happened. Then he gave it a hard kick, something snapped and the car commenced to roll away from the other cars. The car picked up speed as it rumbled downhill to the end of the track where there was a big pile of dirt put there to stop the train in case the brakes failed, or someone like Jake came along.

There was a state highway that crossed the track at the bottom of the slope, and there wasn't a train signal. But shucks, who expected to see a train full of Civil War soldiers come charging out of the woods a hundred some odd years too late?

When that car crossed the highway all the tourists in automobiles were plumb goggle eyed to see a runaway rail car full of Yankees being chased by a dozen yelling Confederates, a couple of hillbillies, two passengers in Hawaiian shirts, and the train crew. By then the car was rolling too fast for the troops to jump, so they rode it out. We picked them all up, dusted them off and checked for broken bones after they hit the pile of dirt and went airborne.

We talked to the tourists while they put the train back together. As we got back on the train we heard a real Yankee from Pennsylvania say to his wife, "My Deah, I told you these Ahkansans were backwahds; they ah still fighting the Civil Wah down heah."

Cousin Jake was so red faced by what he'd done the engineer let him drive the train back to the depot so he'd feel better. Besides, the engineer was a married man, himself.

Now the young'uns all want to go to Little Rock and ride the roller coaster at the State Fair, but Sallie, Sarah and me ain't letting Jake around anything else that runs on rails.

CHAPTER 15
"Henry, the Eighth"
Winter 1981

Jake and I decided to plant more soy beans, so we spent the most part of fall and winter clearing rocks and stumps off the forty acres near the river. While we were clearing we'd roused our share of big, bad snakes. We'd gotten plumb jumpy if we stepped on something that moved.

Sallie Mae had a three year old Rhode Island Red Rooster. She'd had Jake drive all the way to Pine Bluff to buy that rooster when he was still a chick. She called all her roosters, "Henry." As roosters came and went over the years, this one became "Henry, the Seventh." Sallie Mae was proud of the rooster; he'd won a lot of blue ribbons at the State Fair of Little Rock.

Henry and Jake didn't hold with each other, so they tended to stay out of the other's path. Jake tolerated the cantankerous old bird only because Henry and the hens could grow the plumpest, tastiest fryers you ever ate, and Jake fairly loved his fried chicken.

Nobody knows why Henry was under the tree that night, where Jake always parked his pickup, instead of staying in the henhouse with the hens. Jake was plumb worn out from chopping and clearing when he parked the truck and reached for his axe. He was still worried about the wintered down nest of diamondbacks we'd pulled up with some stump roots. He sure hoped none of them got away. Wishing he had a flashlight, Jake stepped out into the dark yard.

Suddenly, something heavy hit his leg above his boot. A terrible sharp pain ran up his leg. "SNAKE," he hollered. He jumped backwards and swung the axe right down where he thought that snake would be, but it wasn't any snake. He had beheaded Henry, the Seventh.

Jake told Sallie Mae as gently as he could. He hoped she wasn't going to cry over a ten dollar rooster. She could get as mad as the other old hens were going to be; he could handle that, but he couldn't hold with seeing her cry.

Sallie got up and walked over to Jake. She hugged him. "Well, it can't be helped," she said. "The old scoot always picked on you; he had it coming to him." She commenced to set the table. "If he'd stayed in the hen house where he was supposed to be instead of sneaking out to jump on you, he'd still be alive. I would have done the same thing you did."

"Maybe I'll get a Wyandotte from Cousin Jim Bob. He says they're easier to keep and have better tempers." She hugged him again. "But I hear they are right costly. Sure hope I've saved enough egg money." She was so understanding that Jake was plumb nervous. The waiting was like an unborn young'un. He knew something was coming, but he didn't know what or when.

Everyone helped their plates. Then Sallie brought a big platter of fried chicken. She gave each child a piece and piled the rest on Jake's plate. "I know you like fried chicken better than anything," she commented, "so you'd better enjoy this tonight. With Ol' Henry gone, there won't be any more fryers." There it was. She wasn't mad, but she was being plumb sarcastic.

Jake took a couple of pieces of chicken and some biscuits and wrapped them in a paper towel. He grabbed his cap and truck keys as he went out the door.

Early the next morning Sallie Mae sat upright in bed when she heard a rooster crowing on the fence outside their window. "What in the world was that?" she asked.

Jake sat up and grinned. "That's Henry, the Eighth. He's a Wyandotte; bought him from Jim Bob last night."

"You're so thoughtful!" She ran to look out the window. "He's so pretty. Look at all them pretty black and white tail feathers. I'm so surprised!" she exclaimed.

Jake chuckled, "You ain't nearly as surprised as them old hens who went to bed with a red rooster last night and woke up with a black and white speckled one this morning."

CHAPTER 16
Riding Lesson
Summer 1982

Jake and Jim Bob decided they each wanted one of those four wheelers. They drove to Texarkana and brought home two big green machines that looked plumb dangerous to me. Their young'uns were tickled pink when Jake and Jim Bob unloaded those pieces of mischief.

Jake told them that he'd have to teach them to ride proper because he didn't hold with broken bones and cracked heads. His lazy yellow speckled dog ran and hid under the house. Jake should have heeded the dog; he was trying to tell him something.

The wives, Jim Bob and I gathered up the young'uns and got into the beds of our pickup trucks. We figured we'd have a better view from up there. Besides, Jake couldn't get to us.

Jake hitched up his overalls and stepped onto his machine. He told us to watch what he did. We studied him real close to learn how he did it. Jake scrunched down on the seat, wiggled around and got comfortable. He fiddled with the knobs and levers on the handles, turned on the key and gave it the gas. That thing roared to life with a mind and will of its own.

Jake destroyed Sallie Mae's rose garden, scattered all the hens,— after he took down the chicken yard fence and snatched all the pretty black and white tail feathers out of Henry, the Eighth.

"They're scared so bad them ol' hens won't lay eggs again for six months!" Sallie shrieked. "And just look what he's done to my rooster!"

"Let up on the throttle!" Jim Bob yelled at him.

Then Jake turned and came by us with tail feathers spinning in the wheels and headed for Sallie's vegetable garden. He was hollering, "WHOA, WHOA—DANG IT—WHOA!"

"Use those brakes!" Sallie Mae hollered.

Jim Bob, Sallie and I bailed out of the trucks and commenced to run after him. Sarah Jane and a dozen young'uns were trailing us.

"Don't you dare run that dang thing through my vegetables!" Sallie Mae screamed. "Use those brakes!"

Jake couldn't hear a word she said over that roaring machine.

"Let up on the throttle!" Jim Bob hollered again.

We chased him through mashed tomatoes and flattened corn stalks, to the back of Sallie's garden, just in time to see him hit the turnip patch.

"TURN LOOSE OF THE THROTTLE!" Jim Bob was getting scared.

"Stay out of them turnip greens!" Sallie hollered. "USE THEM BRAKES!"

"TURN OFF THE KEY AND KILL IT!" I bellowed.

Jake could see our mouths moving, but he couldn't hear a word we were saying. He was glad; he had enough grief right then.

If you've never seen a four wheeler in an acre of turnip greens you've missed a sight. Jake tried turning the wheeler in a circle to keep it away from the highway. We stopped to watch, but all we could see was a cyclone of dust and greens as he straightened up and headed toward Jim Bob's place on the paved road. Jake was dragging corn stalks and purple tops, still hollering, "WHOA!"

Jim Bob had had a lot of misery with folks pushing over his mailboxes. He'd bought an old metal light pole, shortened it, planted it in cement, and welded his mailbox to it. It should have taken an Army tank to knock it over. We watched as Jake and that bad machine mangled a path through Jim Bob's cantaloupe patch, went between the barns and headed for the mailbox post.

While Cousin Jake's broken bones and cracked head mended, Sallie Mae and all the bigger young'uns learned to ride the wheeler, but before they ever got on it, Sallie showed them where the brakes were, what the throttle was for, and if all else failed, how to turn off the key to kill it.

Cousin Jim Bob took his machine back to Texarkana the next day for a refund. Claimed he couldn't afford to lose any more mailboxes.

CHAPTER 17
Pocahontas and Sitting Bull

Summer 1983

Mandy Lee has a full grown Longhorn cow her Pa brought her from Texas. Poca, short for Pocahontas, was a baby heifer when Mandy got her, but she was already ornery. Her bad temper just grew with her.

She was plumb spooky, too. Once, Jim Bob's boy blew up a paper bag and popped it. We found that cow on the other side of Little River County ten days later. It seems we were always looking for her. Every time she ran away, Jim Bob declared it was absolutely the last time. Every time we found her Jim Bob threatened to butcher her. He claimed she ate too much, was a plumb nuisance and wouldn't ever be any use as a milking cow. Then Mandy and the young'uns would all commence to howl and say that she was their pet. Made Jim Bob feel plumb guilty, but he still thought she was a pest.

The day Jake ran that four wheeler across Jim Bob's cantaloupe patch I didn't tell it all. I didn't know it all until later.

Mandy Lee bawled, "When Pocahontas saw that noisy, green monster with headlights that looked like big eyes coming towards our place, she cleared the fence and headed for a new country."

Cousin Jake, the cause of all that commotion, had the easy part. While his broken bones and cracked head mended in the hospital we were all out there hunting that nuisance of a cow for Mandy. We also rebuilt Sallie Mae's chicken yard fence, gathered the chickens, tried to repair her garden and replanted mangled rose bushes. There wasn't anything we could do for Henry, the Eighth; he'd had to grow his own new tail feathers. But that was the start of the story and this is the rest of it.

Mandy declared, "She knew her Pa was really going to like Poca when he saw how big she'd grown. Now what was she going to tell him if he came to visit and the cow was gone?"

Jim Bob told her, "Oh, he's going to like her all right because he's going to have her for breakfast, lunch and supper when he comes to visit again—if I find her!"

I told Jim Bob that he ought to feel plumb ashamed of himself to tease her that way. He stated he wasn't teasing, but to make Mandy feel better, Jim Bob put ads in area newspapers for the missing Poca.

Three weeks passed before a game warden from Oklahoma called Jim Bob and told him there was a huge, red cow with great, long horns, hiding out in Ouachita National Forest. If she was his, would he please come get her because she was being plumb ornery to everyone by chasing campers away from their campsites. .

Mandy insisted on going along that day. She knew the old heifer would come to her if she shook a bucket of feed and called her. Wrong.

Finally the game warden got fed up. He called two rough looking cowboys with cow ponies to come and rope her. Those two cowboys riding cow smart ponies slipped into the woods real quiet like. After awhile we heard yelling, cow bawling, crashing, limbs breaking, thrashing, more yelling and cow bawling. Then the woods got real quiet.

Mandy got into the truck and bawled when Jim Bob said he could taste those steaks. I told him that he ought to be ashamed of himself.

After awhile those two cowboys came across a field from the opposite direction of where they went into the woods. They each had a rope on the horns of the big, red critter and were pulling her between them.

She was ragged and skinny and looked like she'd been dragged through the woods hind end first and horns down; but she was coming along, shaking that big head and bawling. That bad critter was a Longhorn all right: big, red, scrappy, scraggly. But she wasn't Pocahontas. And she wasn't a she. That bad red bull rolled his eyes, tossed his head, roared an indignant bellow, and pawed the ground.

Mandy bellowed, too, "That ain't Pocahontas. That's a bull!" She commenced to wail again.

The game warden said he didn't care if it was Sitting Bull, Mandy could have him if we'd just take him and us back to Arkansas and get out of his woods. When we unloaded Sitting Bull into Jim Bob's corral that night, Pocahontas was plumb glad to meet him.

Seemed my two youngest daughters were berry picking and found

Poca on the back of Jake's place near the lake. They called her and she followed them home gentle as a lamb.

This spring Pocahontas and Sitting Bull had a pretty little red bull calf. Mandy said my girls could have him when he's weaned. They named him "Cochise." It suits him; his horns and bad attitude are already growing. My girls are tickled pink.

I ain't. This is all Jake's fault. If he hadn't brought that four wheeler home that day none of this would have happened.

CHAPTER 18
Citizens' Arrest

Autumn 1984

Jake and I have never understood why people rush out every fall and shoot all the gentle little animals, and sometimes each other. I told him, "They all seem to go crazy for awhile, just like young men when they're chasing purty women."

Jake replied, "The reaction is the same all right, but they don't shoot the women."

Hunting season was right around the corner so Jake and I drove around our farms and checked the "No Hunting" and "No Trespassing" signs nailed up around our fences. Jake declared the deer could hide on our farms until hunting season was over.

Our families loved all creatures and we kept corn and salt blocks near the lake the year around for them. We had bird houses in trees, bluebird houses on fence posts, purple marten houses on tall poles and bird feeders with different seeds for anything that flew. Geese, wood ducks and mallards returned year after year to raise their young'uns on the northeast side of the lake near the tree line.

Over the years our wives and young'uns had raised more orphaned baby animals than we could count. We liked to go hunting with cameras. Sometimes we'd wait for a long time, hidden in a thicket, before a doe and her fawn would slip from the woods to drink from the lake. We'd zoom in with our lens and take several pictures before they'd bound away into the bushes. Our walls were covered with pictures of wild geese and ducks on the lake, possums with babies on their backs, doe rabbits with young bunnies, and every kind of bird we could capture on film.

The day of the arrest, the November weather was sunny and mild, and we were having a picnic at the lake. Sallie and Sarah were throwing a long jump rope and the young'uns were taking turns jumping.

Suddenly we heard shotgun blasts in our woods to the west of us. Jake and I jumped up and commenced to run in that direction. An unharmed picture perfect buck crossed the clearing by the lake and bounded into our woods to the north of us.

Deputy Potter came running into the clearing. He waved his shotgun and hollered, "Did you see which way he went? I think I hit 'im."

Jake grabbed him by the collar, and I jerked his gun away from him. "You're under arrest for hunting on posted property!" Jake shouted into his face.

"You've gotta be kidding." Potter tapped his badge and reared up and gloated hard at Jake and me. "You can't arrest me; I'm the law. I can hunt any place I want."

Undaunted by his badge, we glared back at him.

By then the wives and young'uns had surrounded him. They all shouted at once. Sallie had the coiled jump rope in her hand. They looked like an out of control lynch mob.

Jake shouted, "I'm arresting you with a Citizen's Arrest and you're going to jail right now. You'll learn you can't hunt animals on our land."

Potter eyed the women and young'uns who were closing in on him. "You really ain't joking, are you? But you ain't taking me to jail."

"If you resist arrest I'll give you to them." Jake nodded towards the wives and young'uns who'd moved even closer.

Deputy Potter didn't resist arrest. He didn't speak to us for a long time, but he hasn't trespassed on our property any more either. He's learned that not even the law can hunt on posted property.

CHAPTER 19
Airplane Ride

Summer 1985

Cousin Jake don't hold with no airplanes. He said, "If the Lord wanted me to fly I would have been born with wings. Everything that goes up has got to come down one way or t'other."

Sallie Mae's great uncle had passed away in Phoenix and she was determined to attend his funeral and pay her respects. Jake knew they'd have to go to keep her happy. He also knew his old truck wouldn't get them there in time for the service. Jake weighed his options: the wrath of Sallie Mae for the next six months if they didn't go, or getting on an airplane. He figured, since the airplane couldn't talk, that it was the lesser grief.

Sarah and I kept their young'uns. They packed their bags and drove over to the Texarkana airport. The ticket seller told Jake they'd take a commuter plane to Dallas. Jake thought he said, "computer plane." He refused to get on the plane. He thought there weren't any pilots and it was run by remote control like all those unmanned space capsules.

The ticket seller assured him there were excellent pilots aboard and airplanes were the safest way to travel. He said, "Statistics show you'd have to ride a plane almost every day for nineteen years before you'd be in an accident."

Jake shuffled his feet and looked that agent in the eye. "And what's going to happen if I get on a plane with somebody whose nineteen years is up? The Lord ain't going to pluck just him out of that plane to drop; He's going to drop the whole plane." The ticket seller assured him they had only one chance in ten million of that ever happening.

The flight to Dallas was uneventful. On the way Jake made friends with a salesman, Travis Ware, from Sheridan. Travis was going to Los Angeles for a meeting. They talked about baseball teams and who they thought would play in the World Series that year.

They boarded the passenger jet for Phoenix, and Jake was plumb pleased to find Travis on the flight, too. He could get his mind off being so high above the ground with Travis to talk to. Two days later, after the burying and the meeting, they were all happy to find themselves together again on the flight back to Dallas. A kind passenger exchanged seats with Jake so he could sit next to Travis.

The takeoff was windy and wobbly. Jake's knuckles and face were awfully pale. Jake mentioned to Travis that he could tolerate the flying part of the trip, but he didn't like the shaky take offs and bouncy landings very much. Travis assured him that flying was a piece of cake to him. "Why, I've been flying almost everyday for a long time."

Nervously, Jake inquired, "Just how long have you been flying, Travis?"

Travis unbuckled his seatbelt and leaned back. "Well, let me think." He glanced at the date on his watch and grinned. "Today makes nineteen years I've been a'flyin'."

Jake's heart pounded and he struggled to swallow the lump in his throat. Then he turned and shouted to Sallie Mae across the plane, "START PRAYIN' FOR TRAVIS, HONEY. TODAY HE'S OUR ONE CHANCE IN TEN MILLION!"

CHAPTER 20
Just Between Friends

Summer 1986

A few years ago Jake, Jim Bob and I made a picnic area down by the lake for our families. We hauled in loads of sand for a swimming beach and built some tables near the water. Then we restored the 1880's log cabin that Jake's great grandpa built when he settled the land.

We'd all been at the lake all day one Saturday and it was getting dark. The older young'uns were gathering firewood. They'd talked Jake and me into sleeping in the cabin with them that night, and they wanted to build a campfire to sit around and sing and roast weenies and marshmallows later.

Last spring a thunderstorm blew down a big oak tree growing on the bank. The tree fell into the water near the swimming beach. We'd cut off the branches with chainsaws and dragged them out on the bank, but the huge log still stretched way out into the water. It seems we'd just never got around to bringing the tractor to drag it out.

Jim Bob and his family were gathering their things to go home. He'd promised Mandy and the young'uns he'd take them to see the new Disney movie in Texarkana. Jim Bob came up to Jake and told him, "I just saw a big ol' cottonmouth at the far end of that log over there."

I knew Jim Bob was up to something because I saw the look in his eyes, but Jake didn't notice.

He was busy looking towards the log. He didn't hold with any snakes; especially where the young'uns were swimming.

Jake ventured out on the log, looking for the snake the whole time. About that time, Jim Bob took a long, cane fishing pole and ran it between Jake's feet and wiggled it.

Jake whooped, hollered and shuffled all kinds of dance steps with his arms flapping around like a windmill before he lost his balance and plunged into the lake.

Right then Jim Bob decided it was time to go home.

Jake bobbed around in the water and climbed up the bank. He wrung water from his overalls while he watched Jim Bob's retreating back.

"Might as well go get the tractor," he drawled. "I've been meaning to drag that log out of the water for awhile. Now is as good a time as any."

"What are you fixing to do with that big ol' log when you drag it out, Uncle Jake?" Ben asked.

"Well, just between friends, I'm fixing to give it to Jim Bob for firewood

Twenty feet of uncut firewood was stretched down the middle of his driveway when Jim Bob got home from the movie that night.

CHAPTER 21
"Big, Green 'n Ugly'"
Summer 1987

Jake, Jim Bob and I keep bee hives near the lake on the back of Jake's property. We tend to the bees from time to time and sometimes we get stung. Last year the three of us went to a military auction over near Hooks, Texas. We saw some space suits for sale. Right then we decided that's just what we needed to tend to the bees. The space suits were silvery green with black stripes and had big, round helmets with little knobs and wires poking out all over them. We each bought one. Back at Miss Annie Bea's store we put them on and showed off. Everyone got a big kick out of our space suits.

Jake, Jim Bob and I were having a lot of grief from some city boys who were slipping into the back part of our property to fish and swim in the lake. We didn't mind if they fished and swam; we just wanted them to ask us first. We didn't know who they were, but they left behind trash for us to clean up. Jake set out a metal trash can at the lake with a note on it asking them to use it. A couple of days later Jake and I found the new trash can mashed flat, with a note that said things we couldn't repeat.

Then the trespassers commenced to really destroy things. They ran through fences with their four wheel drive truck and broke down rows of soybeans. Finally they lit a campfire that got away and burned a field of feed corn and Jim Bob's big, new tractor shed. We nailed up "No Trespassing" signs. They'd rip them down, run over them and cut our fences. It got so that all we did was repair their damage and round up livestock.

Sallie Mae, Sarah Jane and Mandy Lee were afraid to take the young'uns picnicking anymore for fear they'd run into those bad people. We're peaceful and generous folks, but enough was enough. We hid in the woods and watched for them, but weren't able to catch them at their mischief.

One Saturday afternoon Jake, Jim Bob and I were getting ready to go to Miss Annie Bea's feed store to play checkers when she called. She told us trouble was headed our way. She said a few minutes earlier three bad boys were in her store getting what they wanted off her shelves, talking nasty and saying they were going swimming. About the time they were walking out without paying for anything, Sheriff Bob Johnson walked in.

When they saw Sheriff Bob, one of them gave Miss Annie Bea a twenty dollar bill. While she made change she winked at Sheriff Bob and asked, loud enough for everyone to hear, "Where have you been, Sheriff Bob? Out looking for those green space aliens again? I hear there's a bunch of them, and I hear they're starting to eat people now!"

Sheriff Bob didn't know what the heck was going on. Around here it could be anything, but he knew Miss Annie Bea was one of the sanest people he knew in the county, so he went along with her story.

"Yep, I'm afraid they're eating folks now. Found some more bones just awhile ago. Picked plumb clean, they were. May never know whose they were." He leaned on the counter and popped open a big R Cee Coler.

The three roughnecks snorted and slammed out the door. They got into their four wheel drive truck laughing and saying something about "crazy rednecks."

Sheriff Bob said he was going to follow them because they were up to no good.

Miss Annie Bea said, "No, just wait here. They'll be back soon. Jake, Jim Bob and Jesse will take care of them."

Wearing our space suits Jake, Jim Bob and I hid in the woods by the lake. We didn't have to wait long before we heard their truck roaring a path through the soybean field. They parked beside the lake and commenced to take off their clothes and toss them on a picnic table. We gave them time to strip to their birthday suits and get into the water before we charged out of the woods, waving big sticks and screeching like banshees.

Those wet, bad boys left everything behind. They fell all over each other getting back in that truck.

Miss Annie Bea said, "When they got back to my store looking for Sheriff Bob, they were butt naked and blubbering like babies about giant spacemen monsters. The boys claimed they were big, green 'n ugly."

Sheriff Bob gave each of them a pair of britches from the lost-and-found box, told them to go home and never come back to his county again.

They were still babbling when they left. Swore the green aliens ripped off their clothes so they could eat them. They were coming out the door of the feed store as Jake, Jim Bob and I went in. They didn't look so bad; just three big, spoilt, overindulged young'uns without enough to do except make mischief. It was a plumb shame to see grown boys wasting their lives and bawling like that.

Sheriff Bob says he doesn't know what we did, and he doesn't want to know, but he sure hopes it was legal, because those boys were a newspaper reporter's son, a doctor's son and a lawyer's son.

Jake, Jim Bob and I just sat back, grinned and commenced to play checkers.

Our community is famous right now. The newspaper reporter has written the story every way his young'un has told it. The stories get better every day. It's the best story he's written since all those Emus got loose in Ashdown.

The lawyer came here to sue somebody, but he couldn't find anybody to sue. He couldn't even find a witness. No one here knows a thing about any big, green and ugly space aliens.

The shrink put his young'un in therapy. He says we all need it, too—whatever that is.

Our tromped down soybean field didn't survive, but we got our money out of it anyway. After we took their knives and guns away from them and gave them all a small stick, we charged all those out of town alien hunters twenty five bucks a head to look for spacemen. We figured they wouldn't hurt each other too bad with the sticks.

A weird group of UFO watchers from Albuquerque wanted to put landing lights in our soybean field inviting the green aliens to land again. They wore hooded dark robes, camped in the woods and carried signs that said, "Welcome to Earth." When our young'uns joined them and started toting signs, we sent our young'uns to the house and the creepy visitors back to New Mexico.

We're ready for things to get back to normal around here. We need to tend to the beehives without getting shot or clubbed to death.

CHAPTER 22
The Lottery

Spring 1988

My cousin, Tom Hatton, and his wife, Ivey, were hard working, God fearing farm folks who'd raised a half dozen young'uns coaxing corn and cotton from a quarter section of Missouri rocks. Sixty years earlier Tommy's father had cleared the land, sawed the trees, planed the lumber and built the clay caulked, clapboard house in which three generations of Hattons had struggled to survive.

Tom and Ivey were strangers to luxury. They went threadbare to send their young'uns, one by one, to college. Now the young'uns were gone and the once crowded house was too large for the two of them. Tom loved the old house where he was born, but he wanted to build a smaller house for Ivey. A house where cold wind didn't blow through cracks in winter, and they could sit in a warm room and watch TV in their old age. That is, if they could save enough money to buy a TV set.

And then, there was Tom's secret lifelong dream that he was certain without a doubt he'd go to his grave without ever realizing. But it was all right to dream about owning just one fancy pickup truck in his lifetime; one with a diesel engine, four wheel drive, lots of chrome, and extra seats for the grand young'uns when they came to visit.

Tom and Ivey were in Texas to attend their youngest child's college graduation when Tom saw the lottery sign in the gas station window. He looked at the precious dollar bill in his hand and passed it to the attendant, "Gimme one of them lottery tickets." Without Ivey knowing, he stood at the counter and carefully selected his numbers—the ages of his six young'uns.

They were staying at a motel in Texarkana when the winning numbers were announced on TV that Saturday night. Tom knew he had all six numbers without looking at his ticket. After all, hadn't he selected his young'uns ages? He was a seven million dollar millionaire. That was the easy part, but there was a hard part, too. How was he going to tell Ivey and the preacher he had gambled?

Ivey took the news with disbelief. First, she found it hard to believe that Tom had gambled. Second, she couldn't believe anyone would give away seven million perfectly good dollars to a complete stranger.

A month passed before Tom and Ivey returned to church. Parishioners stared when Tom parked the brand spanking new black pickup truck, right off the showroom floor. He looked like an undertaker in his new dark suit and tie when he opened the passenger door for Ivey in her finery and offered her his arm. Turned heads and whispers accompanied them to their pew and throughout the service.

After the service Preacher Ezra Jones hurried to the Hattons. He pumped Tom's hand and gushed, "Brother Tom, I'm so glad to hear about your good fortune. I'm sure you'll want to give The Lord His ten percent. Would you be writing Him a check today?"

"No sir," Tom answered. "I got this money by gambling. The devil put me up to it, so I figure it's the devil's money, but I ain't giving the devil his due. I intend to spend it all to make up for the misery the ol' devil has caused my family these many years."

Everyone who was gathered around them gasped. The preacher sputtered.

Tom continued, "For forty years I've written The Lord a check for ten percent every month. There were times I thought about the things my young'uns sorely needed, and I was tempted by the devil to keep that money. But I knew it was The Lord's money, and so I gave it to Him."

The preacher found his voice, "That big, fancy truck must have taken a lot of the devil's money, and you can't take that truck into Heaven with you."

Tom grinned and looked the preacher in the eye. Oh, I know that, Brother Ezra, but I'm sure going to enjoy the ride before I park it outside of them Pearly Gates."

CHAPTER 23
Someone's Worst Nightmare
Winter 1988

Jim Bob and other folks along the county blacktop road were plumb fed up with vandals damaging their mailboxes every Saturday night. The elderly widow, Mrs. Ida Belle Cloud, was indignant at the nasty words they had painted on hers. To calm her, Jim Bob promised that he'd catch the varmints.

Mandy and the young'uns had gone to Texarkana to see a kiddies show at the Little Theater that Saturday night. Jim Bob had begged off going and now the quiet house was getting on his nerves. Nothing good was on TV, and he was bored to death when the thought struck him. Tonight he'd hide in the woods across the road and catch the vandals in the act. He hatched a plan. If he was going to freeze hiding in the bushes, he's make sure the vandals never forgot it.

Jim Bob thought about wearing his silvery green beekeeper spacesuit but remembered that Jake got shot at the last time he wore his. Instead, he put on Mandy's long, furry white bathrobe with a hood and let it hang loose to his feet. Then he took a white garbage bag and cut big round eye holes. He slipped it over his head and immediately yanked it off again when he realized his mistake. "Ain't any mailbox worth smothering for," he grumbled.

Jim Bob cut a big round hole for his mouth and another for his nose to poke through. He slipped it over his head, tied the yellow drawstrings under his chin and pulled up the hood. He looked like someone's worst nightmare.

He put his thermos, ammunition and sandwiches into a plastic grocery sack, grabbed his lawn chair and paint ball rifle and headed across the field towards Jake's house. If anyone saw him, he didn't want to be near his own house and be recognized. By now it was pitch dark. Jim Bob slipped from the field and got to the edge of the blacktop when three cars and an old pickup rounded the curve going to town and caught him in their headlights.

All four came to a screeching halt at the apparition loping across the road carrying a lawn chair, a paint gun and a blue Wal-Mart bag. Then the wide eyed teenagers in the three cars sped away leaving behind Hiram Potter in his noisy old pickup.

"Hey, Jake!" He hollered over the muffler's roar. "What are ya doing? What's going on? What's happening?" Jim Bob raised a hand to wave and disappeared into the woods. Hiram waved back, turned around in the highway and sped back to his grandson's house..

Most people usually didn't believe much Hiram had to say. Like a lot of folks they believed what they wanted to believe, and they'd sure believe this.

Jim Bob laughed out loud. He was glad for the bag over his head. This was better than he'd planned. He still owed Jake a payback for the firewood caper. Tonight he'd kill two birds with one stone. He figured he had an hour before Hiram and Sheriff Bob showed up at Jake's house and another thirty to forty minutes before Jake explained his way out of this one. By then he'd be nice and warm at home.

The night was frosty, but Jim Bob was sweating under the garbage bag. It began sticking to his head and molding around his face in all sorts of grotesque lumps and bumps. He was looking worse by the minute.

A few minutes had passed when he heard four wheelers in the distance. "Probably Jake's and Jesse's young'uns," he mumbled. Then he sat up and took notice when two young'uns stopped at his mailbox. "Deputy Potter's two boys," he muttered. "And they ain't up to any good."

The older boy laughed as he reached for a metal baseball bat and raised it to bash the mailbox. Jim Bob could hear the marble rattling in the can of spray paint the younger boy was shaking..

Jim Bob eased to the edge of the woods, raised the paint gun and fired once, then again, hitting each boy in the back of his thick coat. They both let out loud screams of surprise. Quad reached for his back and drew back a hand covered with red paint. "I've been shot," he screamed. "I'm dying."

Billy stared at his own red hand and whimpered, "I don't want to die!" Both fell to their knees on the blacktop, swaying in agony.

Jim Bob managed to get off four more rounds of paint balls, one on each young'un and one each on the wheelers for identification. Then he let out a loud, keening shriek at their backs that turned their attentions away from their death throes. They turned to look. The worse nightmare they'd ever dreamed was staring down their collars. They'd died for sure and had gone to hell.

Jim Bob chuckled as he watched taillights disappear, "For two young'uns who were mortally wounded they sure got away fast on them four wheelers."

Sarah and I had eaten supper with the Bensons and were kicked back in front of their fireplace. We were watching rented movies on Jake's new big screen television when Deputy Potter banged on the door.

Jake opened the door to face a screaming Trey Potter and his grandpa, Hiram. "My grandpa says he saw you dressed up like a spook and carrying a rifle over on the county road tonight. Now we've just heard on the two-way radio where two young'uns were shot by a lunatic on the county road a while ago. You're under arrest!"

We all stared at the hysterical deputy.

Jake's mouth dropped open. "It's finally happened Trey Potter," Jake shouted back to him. "You've gone as mad as a hatter. If you weren't wearing that uniform I'd smack you good."

Potter stepped back, reached for his gun and realized that he'd forgotten to wear it.

Jake was in his face. "I haven't been out of my house tonight, and I can prove it. And I sure wouldn't shoot a young'un no matter what they'd done. Now get off of my property."

About the time Jake had decided to forget the uniform, another patrol car pulled into his driveway. Sheriff Johnson stepped out and called to Deputy Potter. "Trey, I need to talk to you." He walked to the door and Jake invited them inside to the fireplace. "Trey, someone called me and said he'd caught your two boys destroying mailboxes tonight. Told me he'd shot them and their wheelers with red and yellow paint balls."

Potter sputtered, "Weren't my young'uns. They're rabbit hunting tonight. Seen 'em leave the house myself."

"Oh, they're your boys all right. Caught up with them at your house awhile ago still wearing red and yellow paint smeared from head to tail. They looked like bad modern art. Made them change clothes before they got into my car. I took them back to the mailbox just now and found Quad's baseball bat and Billy's spray can. Oh, they admitted it all right. They're out in the car now."

"Sheriff, arrest Jake! He ain't got any right to run around dressed like a spook and scaring old men and little boys." Hiram shouted.

"Wasn't Jake. About the time all this was happening I was talking to Jake on the telephone about going fishing next Thursday."

Trey Potter glared at me.

"Wasn't Jesse either. I talked to him about fishing, too."

"Then it had to be Jim Bob," Hiram butted in.

"Wasn't Jim Bob either," Sallie snorted. "When I invited them over for supper, Mandy told me they were taking the young'uns to Texarkana tonight."

While all this was going on, a grinning Jim Bob was home alone in his recliner wearing warm pajamas, drinking hot cocoa and watching the ten o'clock news.

CHAPTER 24
"I Saw Daddy Killin' Santie Claus"
Summer 1989

Last Christmas Sarah Jane and Sallie Mae went to Texarkana on a shopping trip. Sarah saw a big stuffed Santie Claus in someone's yard and decided to make one like him for next Christmas.

Sarah sewed on that dummy for nigh onto a week this summer. When she finished his body she stuffed him with quilt batting and painted on a natural looking face. Then she made him a red flannel suit and whiskers of real hair. When she finished him he was taller than me, roly-poly round and looked plumb real.

I got home bone tired one night, and he was leaned back in my recliner with his feet propped up. When I complained Sarah laughed, "If you don't quit grumbling I'll put you on the rooftop next Christmas and keep him. He's taller and better looking anyway; besides, he doesn't complain."

The next morning she dragged him into my workshop and stuffed him onto a shelf. Several times a day for a week I shoved Santie Claus back into the shelf. He just wouldn't stay where we put him. Finally I got fed up one night and dragged him across the field to the big hay barn and put him on the shelf by the door. I turned off the barn light and went to Jake's back door to tell him what I'd done.

Sallie Mae met me at the door. "Jake just called from Jim Bob's. He saw a light in the big barn and is checking on it before he comes home."

Before I could tell her that it was me in the barn, their littlest young'un came up the trail screaming, "Mama, Mama, come quick! I just saw Daddy killing Santie Claus!"

Sallie froze to the porch, and I commenced to run towards the barn. Halfway there I met Jake charging towards the house and roaring like a bull, "Some big idiot in a Santie Claus suit attacked me just as I opened the barn door. I knocked him out plumb cold. Go watch him while I call the sheriff!" He kept on running towards the house.

I was laughing so hard I could hardly drag Santie Claus back to my workshop to hide him. Sheriff Johnson and Deputy Potter came. We all searched high and low. There was nary a trace of Jake's attacker.

By then Cousin Jake was convinced that it was an escaped maniac. "Who else would run around in a hot Santie Claus suit in the middle of July?" He stomped around grumbling and searched for clues. It was all I could do to keep from busting out laughing.

Jake didn't think it was funny when Deputy Potter grinned and commented, "Maybe Santie Claus just came to count all these young'uns for next Christmas."

Since July that Santie Claus maniac, who was never caught, has been blamed for every foul deed that's happened in the county. When Jerome Parson's wife come back home, she said she was kidnapped by the maniac, but everyone knows she ran off with that funeral insurance salesman from Texarkana.

Then Ol' Pit turned up missing. Horace swore the maniac took him. Horace found him a week later at Hiram Potter's house visiting a lady dog.

Even Sallie Mae got in on it. Her hens kept disappearing until Jacob found a fox in the hen house one night.

The Saturday afternoon stories in Miss Annie Bea's feed store get wilder and better. It's bigger than the UFO alien sightings we had a couple of years ago. It seems everyone has glimpsed the maniac at some place or other—still wearing his red suit. Jake believes them all.

Miss Annie Bea says that she's going to write a book about us when she retires. Horace and Jim Bob said to leave them out of it; they think we're all seeing things, but Horace did declare he saw one of the aliens last year and took a shot at him.

I just grin and play checkers. I'll never tell on Jake, but I can't wait to see his face when he spots that maniac sitting on my rooftop next December.

CHAPTER 25
Ol' Pit

Autumn 1990

A few weeks ago Cousin Jake went out and bought himself a set of those big, shiny round hubcaps. They were awfully expensive and everybody thought it was plumb foolishness. Jake was right taken with them. He boasted, "There ain't any more like them in three counties."

We were all sitting around talking and playing checkers in Miss Annie Bea Teal's feed store like we do every Saturday afternoon. Horace Smith wasn't there that day so we commenced to talk about his sneaky mean, truck chasing bulldog, Ol' Pit. That bulldog was meaner than a rattler and a plumb nuisance to everybody. We'd get to rolling down the hill on that gravel road in front of Horace's house and that ol' bulldog would run out in front of our trucks and make us slam on our brakes or run into the ditch to keep from hitting him. After we stopped he'd try to eat the tires off our wheels.

We never knew where he was coming from. One time he'd be hiding in the woods. The next time he'd come from the neighbor's barn across the road. Sometimes he hid under the bridge like a grumpy old troll. Harvey Dockins jackknifed his hay trailer and lost his load of hay one day when Ol' Pit charged at him from under the bridge. One of the Johnson boys ran his loaded log truck into the ditch to keep from hitting him after he came from the woods.

Ol' Pit especially didn't like Jake's truck wheels because he thought that mean snarling dog he was seeing in those bright, shiny hubcaps wanted to fight him. He'd scratched Jake's fine, new hubcaps something terrible trying to whip that other dog.

The stories went on and on. We were all plumb fed up with that useless dog. Then Jim Bob said he'd heard of a man who broke a dog from chasing cars by tying an old britches leg to the wheel and letting that bad dog grab hold as he drove past. A few flips on a rocky road broke that dog of his bad habit. Everyone listened real close.

While he drove the six miles to get home that Saturday, Jake studied about what Jim Bob had told them. He chuckled to himself. Horace's house was just under the hill. Jake stopped his truck and stepped out. Jake had worn a pair of ragged, worn out overalls that day so he could help his little sister, Becky Sue, load sacks of horse feed into her truck. He took his pocket knife and cut a leg off the overalls he was wearing. Then he took pieces of hay strings and tied the britches leg to the left rear hubcap real good.

He could hear Ol' Pit raising sand down the road; barking like crazy, just waiting for him. Jake adjusted the outside mirror so he could see the rear wheel, got into his truck and gunned it towards Horace's house. Jake said Ol' Pit saw those shiny hubcaps and the britches leg coming towards him going a-flippity-flop as the wheels turned. It was like waving a red flag in front of a big, bad bull.

First time Jake looked back he saw Ol' Pit turning flips on the gravel road. He was all wound up in the britches leg and hollering like he was mortally wounded. Then Jake thought he saw something else; he stopped to look back again. That sneaky ol' dog had pulled off his hubcap with the britches leg and was taking it home with him. Jake would never live this one down.

He didn't mention the missing britches leg or the hubcap when he got home that night. Sallie wasn't surprised at anything he did anymore, but it was only a matter of time before a young'un noticed the hubcap missing and said something at the supper table. Wives and young'uns have a way of bringing up things at the supper table to spoil a man's appetite.

There wasn't any sign of Ol' Pit the next morning on the way to church. Sallie Mae commented, "Someone must have finally run over him the way he chased them cars and all. He certainly had it coming to him. Sure had a nasty disposition."

Jake commenced to worry; he hadn't meant to kill him, just teach him a lesson. A week passed and still there was no sign of Ol' Pit or the hubcap. Jake mustered the courage to mention the dog to Horace at the feed store.

Sallie Mae and Frannie Faye stood nearby and listened, smiling at each other. Miss Annie Bea grinned and winked at the ladies. She was like some of those politicians: she heard everything, but she didn't know a thing.

"Oh, he's all stove up," Horace commented. "It's a real mystery whet happened to him. Must have got himself run over last weekend. Come to the house all whining—limping—dragging a britches leg tied to a hubcap. And he ain't chased no more cars. Acts like he's brooding—studying about something—planning his next move." Horace watched Jake real close.

Jake shuffled his feet and jingled keys and coins in his pockets. He tossed a couple of quarters on the counter and took a big R Cee Coler from the cooler. He thought it was getting plumb warm in there.

Horace went on. "All he does is lay in his dog house and guard them britches legs. Can't figure out where he got 'em all. And why in the world would anyone tie a britches leg to a hubcap?"

Jake's face turned bright red and the R Cee Coler went down wrong.

Sallie and Frannie made it outside before they busted out laughing. Seems the wives were plumb puzzled last Sunday morning to learn some of their men folk came home the evening before with a britches leg missing. They talked about it all week and by the time Thursday's choir practice came around they'd imagined some pretty wild tales. One by one they told their stories.

Then Frannie Faye (who never liked her husband's bad dog anyway) told them what really happened. She'd watched out the window for Horace to come home and saw it all. Sarah told me later the ladies couldn't sing for laughing. She giggled, "Becky Sue sure had an evil grin when Millie Johnson commented that the men folks have all the fun."

I just wish Sarah hadn't found my britches that I hid in the woodpile. She hollered, "I always thought you were smarter than the average hillbilly, but that's what I get for letting you run loose with Jake and Jim Bob. They're bad influences—both of them!" She shook her head and busted out laughing, "At least you didn't lose your hubcaps when you lost all your good sense!"

Next Saturday, on his way to town to play checkers, Jake saw Ol' Pit sitting by Horace's front gate. Jake's hubcap was hanging on the fence beside the dog. Ol' Pit snarled at him as he drove by. Jake knows, that everybody else knows, that that's his hubcap hanging on Horace's fence with the britches leg still attached. He won't live this down for a long time.

Jake figures he'll get his hubcap when the dog dies of old age. Besides, the old nuisance earned it. There were seven folks in the feed store who drove past Horace's house going home that evening. Jake was the last one. That tough old bulldog must have turned a lot of flips before he finally got the prize.

CHAPTER 26
Melon Mashin'

Summer 1991

Sheriff Bob grumbled, "What are those three doing now," when he heard a truck screech to a halt in front of Miss Annie Bea's feed store. He knew that Jake, Jim Bob and I were probably up to something because we weren't there that Saturday afternoon, and he knew we loved to play checkers.

Hiram Potter ran into the store yelling, "Sheriff Bob, you've gotta come quick—watermelons is fallin' outta the sky at my place! One done hit my mule—knocked him out plumb cold, it did!"

Everybody knew that Hiram made a little corn licker on the side. Sheriff Bob couldn't find a still, but he knew there had to be one somewhere, because nobody just naturally acted like Hiram. He was always hearing voices or seeing things, but this time maybe he had a reason to jump around waving both arms.

Yesterday, Sheriff Bob had wondered why Jake drove all the way to Hope to buy a pickup load of culled watermelons; now he thought he had the answer. He sighed and turned to Miss Annie Bea, "Call the folks out on the ol' Benson place and find out what they're doing this afternoon. I can't imagine what they're doing—and probably don't want to know—but somehow, I think Jake Benson's name is on those melons. I'm going out there."

Miss Annie Bea laughed and commenced to dial the phone.

By the time Sheriff Bob got here, we'd hidden the catapult behind stacks of hay in the big barn and were quietly cleaning out stalls in another barn.

A couple of weeks earlier Jake saw a program on his big screen TV that showed some good ol' boys up North having an event called a "Punkin Chunkin'" They were using catapults and seeing who could toss them pumpkins the farthest The prize money was almost as much as we made on crops in a year. Besides, it looked like fun. Now, it ain't good to plant ideas into Jake's head, because it don't take long for them little seeds to grow into something.

Cousin Jake figured he could do anything them Yankees could do and probably better. Since Arkansas ain't exactly known for its pumpkins, he decided to chunk watermelons instead. He decided he'd have an annual event right there on his place and call it a "Melon Mashin'," but first he had to build himself one of those catapults and learn how to use it. He wanted it big and powerful.

When Jake asked Jim Bob and me to help him build it, Mandy Lee wailed, "The first time one of them melons flies over Pocahontas' head, she'll jump the fence and be leaving!"

Sallie muttered that she and the young'uns might be leaving, too.

Jake assured us that all his practice shots would be aimed towards the five acres down by the creek. Later, we all remembered those words.

On the day of the first test flings our boys Jimmy, Ben and Jacob were down at the creek to see where our shots landed. We'd flung a half dozen melons before Ben raced back to us hollering, "Those melons are flying plumb out of sight across the creek." Across the creek were Hiram's place, Horace's place and our little Congregational Methodist Church.

As it happened, that was the Saturday of the month that the ladies got together at the church house and prepared clothing for the needy. They'd spent all day mending and washing and ironing all those clothes real nice. They'd laid them out on tables by the wall and were getting ready to sort them into sizes when an oversized and overripe melon crashed through the window and smashed into the wall, flinging juice everywhere.

All the ladies screamed.

Old Miss Potter shrieked, "It's the work of the devil."

Sallie Mae yelled, "It's the work of Jake Benson, and we're going to kill him!" Christian charity was left behind when fourteen juice covered women stormed out of that church house. Those ladies were all hell bent on murder. It was a good thing that Sheriff Bob and Deputy Potter got to our place the same time as those women.

Sheriff Bob couldn't find anything in his book about flying melons. There just wasn't anything that said a melon was a weapon. They weren't really guided missiles; he couldn't use that against us. They weren't discharged from any firearm, so it wasn't an act of war. By the time he'd read through his book, he'd realized that he couldn't even fuss at us. He couldn't figure out how we were throwing melons on t'other side of the creek and cleaning barns at home at the same time; but he knew we done it. By the time he got into his patrol car and drove away, he'd chewed plumb through his pipe stem.

Hiram Potter doesn't make corn licker anymore. When a hard, green melon found his well hidden whiskey still in the middle of a hundred acres of woods, he figured it was God's Hand guiding it. As it turned out, Hiram's mule wasn't hit by a melon. He'd just keeled over dead drunk from eating sour mash when the still was busted.

Later, Horace Smith mourned, "Ol' Pit had been run over by big trucks, shot a few times and snake bit more times than he could count. He was a tough ol' bulldog. Who would have ever thought a watermelon could kill him?"

Jake, Jim Bob and I replaced the window at the church house with a stained glass window the ladies had always wanted. It was a picture of Jesus thrashing the devil. Sallie Mae said one of those fellows looked like Jake—and it wasn't Jesus. Sallie Mae is still mad at Jake. He ain't had any fried chicken since all that happened.

CHAPTER 27
The Climb to Great Heights

Autumn 1991

William Bryant Adams, the Fourth, and Thomas Gibson Adams were two young'uns who'd spent most of their young lives making mischief. Anything those brothers thought of, they did it.

The young'uns were left in the care of their parents' housekeeper and gardener, Bessie and Alton Morrow, who'd lost control years ago. Those boys weren't really bad, just creative. They'd done things like rolling trees with toilet paper and pouring Super Suds in the town fountain.

Once they spent all weekend catching a feed sack full of chicken snakes. Monday morning the boys turned the snakes loose in the hallway at the middle school. Then they hid and shook the snake rattles they'd bought at a flea market. Everybody was already outside by the time the principal got to the intercom to evacuate the building.

School was closed for a week while volunteers rounded up all those snakes. I didn't help; I don't hold with any snakes.

The boys painted big hot pink and purple polka dots on Wesley Potter's prize pigs just before the State Fair at Little Rock. The pigs didn't win anything, but they sure got the most attention. One night they slipped into Horace's pasture and painted the word "COW" in huge, white letters on the sides of all his nice Black Angus heifers. Willie and Tommy told Horace they were protecting them from hunters and were saving him the trouble.

About the meanest thing they ever did was shaving Miss Annie Bea's toy poodle, Fluffy. Poor embarrassed little Fluffy ran home crying and looking like a peeled possum. Miss Annie grabbed her broom and almost killed him for a varmint before she recognized him. Miss Annie threatened those boys with horrible deaths and meant every word. Old Brother Cummings talked to Miss Annie about forgiveness. She declared that she'd forgive them when all of Fluffy's hair grew back, and she'd sure better not see those boys before then. The boys stayed out of her sight for a long time.

Willie and Tommy were always just one step ahead of Sheriff Bob who really worried about them. He'd talk to them, and they'd straighten up for a week or two before they'd revert to their old tricks.

Their Pa, William B. Adams III, was a politician in Little Rock. Sometimes he and their Ma came home on weekends if they weren't flying off to some party or another. Every time Sheriff Bob got in touch with him about the boys' capers, all their Pa would say was, "Boys will be boys. Ain't they smart to think of all them clever things to do? My boys are going to climb to great heights and really clean up one of these days!"

Sheriff Bob could never catch them at any of their pranks. He couldn't do anything if he did. They hadn't really hurt anything. Most folks just shook their heads at the aggravation, cleaned up their messes and went on.

But some folks were plumb fed up with the boys, and Jake and I were, too. We just didn't hold with that kind of mischief. Halloween was just around the corner and we'd cleaned toilet paper from our trees after the last two Halloweens. That year we hid in the bushes and waited for them.

Late on Halloween night Jake called their Pa in Little Rock. He listened patiently to the politician's usual recitation about his talented sons climbing to great heights and really cleaning up some day.

Then Jake politely assured him. "Well, Mister Senator Adams, tonight they both got their chances. They've climbed to great heights. Now as we speak, William has climbed to the top of my tallest pine tree. He's cleaning up the toilet paper they unrolled tonight. And Thomas has climbed a ladder onto Jesse's second story roof. He's scrubbing off all the eggs they threw at Jesse's house. Yes sir, Mister Senator Adams, I'd say they have climbed to great heights and are really cleaning up. Goodbye, Mister Senator Adams. Have a good night."

CHAPTER 28
Funny Stuff

Summer 1992

One day Jake and I were checking the timber on the far side of our property. This is acreage where we seldom go because all it does is grow big pine trees that we sell to the paper mill every few years.

We were walking along talking about fishing, wives, young'uns and other things when we came across a well worn trail into the woods. The trail had been well hidden by somebody who'd covered it with cut brush.

"Now, who do you think made this trail and tried to hide it?" Jake wondered.

"Let's follow it and find out." I answered him.

"Do you think we should? Whoever did this sure doesn't want anyone to know what they're doing. Do you think they're making corn licker in there? Some of them bootleggers can get plumb mean" Jake added, "Maybe we ought to get Sheriff Johnson."

We sniffed the air. We couldn't smell mash brewing or see drifting wood smoke. "More than likely they're poaching deer." I answered. "Let's check it out." My curiosity had gotten the best of my good sense.

We slipped into the woods and tip-toed down the trail very quietly. It wasn't long before we heard someone talking low and making cranking sounds. Jake and I got down and crawled through the bushes and peeked towards the sounds.

We were plumb shocked at what we saw! There were two of them tending to weeds! They'd put a hand pump in the creek and had a proper irrigation system with ditches and pipes. One ol' boy was up at the creek working the pump handle while another one was making sure all the plants got watered. And those plants—why, there were dozens of them growing higher than Jake's head, and Jake is a tall man. Whatever the ol' boys were doing, they were really serious about it, because they were wearing guns in shoulder holsters and had shotguns within reach. They were big time bad and they weren't from around these parts. . .

Then we heard a bird whistle behind us that wasn't any bird we'd ever heard before. There was a third man, a lookout. He must have glimpsed us slipping through the woods. It wasn't ten seconds until the others were gone. They'd just melted into the thickets like ghosts.

Jake and I hunkered down into thick bushes, scared half to death. We were afraid to whisper or even breathe. We just knew they could hear our knees knocking and our teeth chattering. Jake and I waited a quarter hour, scared the whole time. We were woodsmen and knew our ways around the woods, so we slipped out of the bushes and decided to split up. If they got one of us, the other would live to tell what happened. We agreed to meet back at the lake where we'd left the truck. We told each other to be real careful because neither of us is hero material.

I studied on those outlaws while I was slipping out of the woods and decided they were growing that funny tobacco we'd heard about. When we met at the truck I told Jake that we had to get the sheriff real quick.

"I don't know about that." He fretted, "What'll he say about all that funny stuff growing on our property if we tell him?"

"What will he say about that funny stuff growing on our property if someone else finds it and tells him first?" I answered him.

Jake studied on that for a minute, hitched up his overalls and said, "Let's drive into town."

When we got back to the woods Sheriff Johnson told us that was one of the finest crops of marijuaner he'd ever seen in this county. Then he and Deputy Potter commenced to chop it down to put it in a big pile. After awhile they tossed on some fuel and set the pile ablaze.

Sallie Mae says she's worried about Jake. "He ain't done anything' for two days except walk around giggling. He acts plumb silly, kind of childish, you know."

I told her that he'd be all right in a day or two. Sure wish he'd listened to us, though. We all told him not to stand in the smoke.

CHAPTER 29
Aren's Cross

Spring 1993

Sarah and I were enjoying a quiet supper with Jake and Sallie. Our young'uns were scattered to different places. Ben and Beth were attending the university in Texarkana. Jacob was in school at Magnolia and Little Alice was studying in Arkadelphia.

My twin girls, Charley and Vicky and Jake's daughter, Jenny, were at the young people's church supper and choir practice. My youngest, five year old Sammy was eating his hotdog in front of the TV in Jake's den.

Jake's youngest son, Aren, had taken a job at the new burger place in town. He was scheduled to work until midnight on his first night so we were surprised to see him walking through the back door. He had a mournful face.

"Why are you home so early, Son?" Jake asked.

"Manager told me they couldn't use me, Dad. She said I didn't fit in."

"Why?"

"Some kids came into the place. They were saying bad things about Jesus. Really bad things; cursing and using His name in vain. Thought they'd leave after awhile, but they just went on and on saying those bad things."

"What happened then?"

We all listened to the sad young'un.

"I stood it as long as I could, and then I took up for Him. Told them I didn't want to hear any bad mouthing about Jesus. Said I didn't want to hear His name used in vain."

"I'm proud of you, Son." Sallie smiled.

Aren looked toward his mother. "The manager heard me, Mama."

"And then?"

"She fired me. The trouble makers all laughed. They called me a

'Jesus freak.'" Aren wiped his eyes and looked at his dad. "It isn't fair, Daddy. I took up for Jesus and lost my job."

Jake left the supper table. He wrapped comforting arms around his young son and hugged him. "You did right. And Son, you got off easy. When Jesus took up for you, He lost His Life."

CHAPTER 30
Cement Mixer

Summer 1993

With all things considered, Gerald Walker is a pretty good ol' boy although none of our wives will have anything to do with him anymore. Three years ago Gerald, who was an elder in our church, went middle aged crazy and left his wife, Clara Jean, and four young'uns.

He'd met Sherry, a lady of the night (and day), at a truck stop at Winnsboro.. She was younger than his daughters. He married Sherry and bought her the big, fancy house she demanded in an expensive new housing addition.

He soon learned that Sherry had never been to a church service and didn't plan to start going, so Gerald stopped going. This set the already wagging tongues in the community to flapping at both ends.

At our Saturday afternoon checker games we ribbed Gerald and told him to store plenty of ice water because he'd need it where he was going.

He hooked his thumbs under his suspenders, leaned back in his straight chair grinning and bragged, "It'll be worth it to shovel those buckets of hot coals later. I'm already in Heaven and all those clouds are lined with pure gold."

"Huh! There's no fool like an old fool," Miss Annie Bea muttered. While she listened to him, she scrubbed that counter top until the paint peeled.

As the Saturdays passed Gerald became quieter and sadder. It appeared to us the gold lined clouds had started to tarnish. We'd heard rumors that Sherry had wandering eyes that really enjoyed traveling.

Gerald drove a cement truck for a Texas construction company. The owner, Buddy Davis, was a good and fair man, but Bud decided to sell the business and enjoy the fruits of his years of hard labor.

The new owner, Lee Roy Snipes, was a self-centered northerner. He'd come to Texas to show all them snake stompers how to run a business. Soon he'd made lots of changes and even more enemies.

Lee Roy went to Dallas and bought himself a big, fancy convertible car. He added Holstein cowhide—hair and all—seat covers and a pair of long horns, minus the cow, as hood ornaments. To complete his new image he headed to a western wear store and bought embroidered shirts and tight jeans. They made him a silver trimmed black belt with "Lee Roy" on the back. He added black, silver toed size thirteen-and-one-half boots and topped this outfit with a huge hat with a rattlesnake band. It was plumb unnerving to see that stuffed snake's head staring at us over the brim of that hat.

Every evening Sherry picked Gerald up after work. She sat in her silver sports car and flirted with his co-workers, who ignored her. Lee Roy noticed her the first day, and she noticed him. He was a lot older than she liked her men, but she could smell money a mile away.

The boss strolled over to the car. This was his kind of woman. They both used words from the gutter and liked to stay out all night drinking and making whoopee. Those two were the kind that made all Texans look bad, and they weren't even from Texas.

Gerald's friends ribbed him about Sherry and the boss. Then they whispered behind his back.

Soon they avoided him altogether and glanced his way with pity. Things at home began to change, too.

She was too tired to cook anymore and the house was always cluttered. He found cigarette butts in the ashtrays that weren't the brand Sherry smoked. Then Gerald noticed that Lee Roy always left the job site as soon as he got to work in the mornings.

Everything came to a head the morning Gerald got into his loaded cement truck with that rotating mixing drum. He was headed to a messy street job in his own subdivision. He swung by his house to get an extra set of work clothes in case he got cement on the ones he was wearing.

Lee Roy's big, fancy red convertible was parked at the end of his driveway.

Gerald's past raced before his eyes when he thought of all he'd lost for a harlot. Many times he'd regretted his decision when he missed Clara Jean and their young'uns who all refused to have anything to do with him. He couldn't blame them a bit; he didn't like himself much either.

The new street they were pouring was at the top of the hill. Gerald could see all his co-workers watching him. Gerald wasn't a violent man, but his reputation was at stake. A man had to do what a man had to do. He backed the giant rumbling truck to the red convertible and lowered the cement chute into the back seat.

His friends all cheered.

Gerald flipped the switch and walked toward his friends on the hilltop. Hairy black and white seat covers disappeared under a rush of the gray mixture. From the hilltop his friends jumped up and down and cheered. The back of the car filled and seeped into the front. Soon gray mush oozed from the filled car onto the street and still the cement came.

The neighbors left their houses to see what was happening. Amazed, they all stood around it and watched. Before long there was only a hardening gray lump with two cow horns sticking out.

Lee Roy left his boots and embroidered shirt at Gerald's house that day when he slipped out the bedroom window. He didn't return for them before he went back to New York. Sherry didn't go with him. She went back to where ever she came from. The ladies have their theories that I won't repeat.

Gerald is the local hero. Now he drives the cement truck for the new owner: himself. The banker declared that a man with that kind of guts could make the business pay. He loaned Gerald the money to buy it after the bank foreclosed on Lee Roy.

His young'uns all think he's the coolest person they know. Clara Jean forgave him but she wouldn't have him back. She vowed that forgiveness is one thing but forgetting is another. Besides, she and his former boss are enjoying Buddy's retirement.

CHAPTER 31
Ol' Bullet

Spring 1994

Jake's Pa gave us his fat brown mule, Ol' Bullet, when we moved to the farm. Luther had named him "Bullet" because he was so slow he'd almost fall asleep pulling the plow. But Bullet was dependable, he was strong and he knew how to get the work done.

Bullet was a good babysitter as the kids came along and grew. He was gentle and loved their attention. They'd ride him around the yard with nothing but a rope halter. He'd step along as softly as a ballerina with four or five young'uns on his back. If one slipped off, he waited until the young'un climbed on again. Bullet was like a member of our families.

Soon after he came to our place Bullet learned to open doors and gates. He'd come to the kitchen door and wait for a handout. He ate anything. If it came from someone's hand he considered it a treat. His favorite food was Sarah's cornbread. She'd stand on the back steps and call, "Hooooo, Bullet, come get your cornbread. Here's cornbread, Bullet; come get your cornbread." Didn't matter where he was, we'd soon hear his hoof beats trotting around the house.

Jake commented, "That's the fastest I've ever seen Ol' Bullet move. Do you think Sarah could run along in front with a pan of cornbread while we plow?"

A mule isn't like a horse that will eat himself to death. A horse will eat as long as there's something in front of him to eat, then he'll colic, founder or die. Mules know when they've had enough and will walk away before they get sick.

We didn't worry about him when he went to the apple and peach orchards. He'd eat the windfalls but wouldn't touch the fruit on the trees. During harvest time he'd wait in harness and pull the wagon from tree to tree while we gathered fruit to carry to our roadside stand. Every summer folks came to pick their own peaches from the orchards. We'd hitch Bullet to the wagon and he'd take them to the orchard. He'd wait for them to pick their peaches and then brought them back to the fruit shed. He never lost a peach or a picker. Soon he became a local celebrity.

Back in the days when R Cee Coler came in a bottle, Bullet would turn up a bottle and chug a lug it down. When pop-top cans came along Bullet couldn't quite get the hang of drinking from one. Then Sarah thought to pour his R Cee Coler into a bottle for him. That worked just fine.

One day Hiram Potter came over with some of his corn licker in a long necked bottle. He gave it to Bullet who turned it up and then spewed it all back on Hiram. Sarah bristled, "Serves you right! He doesn't want your corn licker; he's a good Methodist mule!"

Modern equipment took his place as the years passed. The young'uns grew up and Bullet got older. He wandered around the homesteads missing the young'uns and mooching handouts at back doors. He spent most of his time in the big barn. Sallie and Sarah carried his favorites to him every day: raisins, chopped apples and cornbread.

Jake and I were driving on Interstate 30 coming home from a farmers' meeting in Arkadelphia when we heard about the tornado. Our county had taken a hit. We commenced to fret when the announcer mentioned the hardest hit area was the Benson Community in the western part of the county. We pulled into a truck stop and tried to call home, but the phone lines were down. We got back to the truck and sped home as fast as we could through blinding rain.

Rain was still falling in sheets when we rushed into our driveway. Everything seemed all right until we looked towards the big barn that was flat on the ground. Our families and neighbors stood around looking at it.

"Where are the animals?" Jake hollered.

Sheriff Bob shouted back, "They all got out before the storm hit; all except Ol' Bullet. He's still in there."

Sarah, Sallie and Mandy stood together bawling their eyes out. Jim Bob looked plumb miserable himself. I knew how he felt. We all hugged the girls and I told them, "There's nothing we can do for him now in this rain. Let's all go home and get some warm, dry clothes and drink some hot coffee. Later Jake, Jim Bob and I will move the boards with the tractor and find him. Then we'll all give him a proper burial."

Sarah wailed, "He didn't get his cornbread today."

A couple of hours had passed. Sarah and I sat in front of the television talking and watching the news about the storm damage. We couldn't figure out how the livestock got safely out of the barn before the storm struck. Bullet was the only animal who could open the doors and he was still in there.

Sarah went to the kitchen to check on the cooking supper when I heard her scream, "Jesse!"

Heart pounding, I raced into the kitchen.

Bullet stood with his head through the open kitchen door happily munching on cornbread. Sarah was draped around his neck and kissing that ol' brown mule. I felt like it, too.

"Don't you see?" she shouted. "Before the tornado hit he let all the other animals out of the barn when he came to the house looking for his cornbread. He's a hero; he saved their lives. He rode out the storm by the kitchen door."

That night I ate store bought white bread with my fried taters, pinto beans and ham hocks, but it was all right. Sarah had fed Ol' Bullet the whole skillet of cornbread.

CHAPTER 33
Calculations
Autumn 1994

Aren, Jake's youngest child, remarked to his dad at the supper table, "I need twenty bucks for a new calculator, Dad."

Jake made a quick mental check: he'd bought Aren a new calculator when school started two weeks ago. "What happened to yours?"

"Some kid stepped on it at school today. It's totaled."

Jake was interested. "How did some kid step on it?"

"I dropped it and he stomped it before I could pick it up."

"Why would he do something like that? We wouldn't have destroyed a classmate's belongings for anything when I was a kid."

Aren knew he was about to get a lecture. "Things have changed since you were in school, Dad. Some kids are just bad that way."

Jake sighed at his young son. He really worried about teenagers today: what they were learning in school; what they weren't learning; and what they were learning that they shouldn't be learning.

He reached around to his back pocket for his billfold. "And we didn't use store bought calculators either. We had our own kind; best in the world. Carried them with us everywhere we went. Came in right handy, too; we couldn't drop them."

"Really? Cool! Where can I get one of those kinds, Dad?"

"You already have one, Son. You were born with it. I don't know what you young'uns call it today, but my generation called it 'our brain.'"

CHAPTER 34
Tadpole Johnson

Spring 1995

Jake and Sallie Mae have a pretty little girl named, "Nancy Alice." Little Alice, as we call her, has long, silvery blond hair growing below her waistline and big, blue eyes. She's the image of Jake's Ma, but definitely has a mind of her own.

The last two years that she was in high school Brother Cummins was a regular visitor to Jake's house. He was fresh out of preaching school and ours was his first church. He'd grown up in our community. His pa and grandpa were both preachers. Jake knew the two young'uns liked each other and talked about getting married some day so Jake had gotten used to the idea of having him for a son-in-law.

Just before her high school graduation Little Alice told her folks that she'd gotten a scholarship to Arkadelphia. She'd gotten a calling to spread the gospel and wanted to be a lady preacher.

Brother Cummins protested, "Lady preachers aren't allowed in our denomination, and besides, he aimed to marry her and one preacher in the family was enough."

Alice answered him, "Well, I won't marry you then, and I'll join the church over in Texarkana where they do have lady preachers!" She did just that. An uneasy summer passed. Then Little Alice, with her mind still made up, packed and moved into the dormitory in Arkadelphia.

All heck broke loose at Jake's house. Sallie and the girls took sides with Alice while Jake and the boys sided with Brother Cummins. Soon afterwards, Brother Cummins moved to a church in Fort Smith and they didn't hear from him again.

Little Alice was in her third year at the university when she called her parents and asked if her boyfriend could visit during the Easter break. They had dated for a year, were in love and engaged to be married. She wanted them to know him. Alice would come home earlier in the week and he would come for the Easter weekend.

Sallie Mae was happy for her but Jake was upset. His little girl was marrying a total stranger from way off somewhere that he didn't know a thing about. Why his family could be bootleggers, murderers, drug dealers or worse still—Yankees! Jake fretted so much that he made himself and everyone else miserable.

The day before Easter we were all in Miss Annie Bea's store playing our Saturday afternoon checker games. A tall, tow headed young man come into the store and bought an R Cee Coler. He leaned on the counter and drank it while he watched us play checkers.

Jim Bob asked him, "Would you care to play checkers with us, Stranger? You're sure welcome to play if you'd like."

The young man set his empty can on the counter and answered, "If y'all don't mind, I'd sure enjoy a game or two. I haven't played checkers since I was a little boy." Horace had to leave early that day so the young stranger took Horace's chair across from Jake. He shook Jake's hand and said, "I'm Tad."

Now Jake was the checker champ of the county but it wasn't long before he knew that he'd met his match. Time after time Jake and the grinning young man exchanged wins. By then Jake was getting real fond of the pleasant young man. He'd learned his Pa was minister of music and assistant pastor at a church in Jonesboro. The boy's Momma and two older sisters were school teachers, and the boy was studying to be a game warden or a forest ranger. He hadn't quite decided which. The young man thanked Jake for the checker games and talked with Miss Annie Bea for a few minutes before he left.

"Now, that was a well raised young'un," Jake told his friends. "He was just like us. He was as country as collard greens and cornbread. Why didn't my Little Alice find herself a nice young man like that one instead of some stuck-up Yankee from way off somewhere?" Jake turned to Miss Annie Bea. "I didn't hear his last name. Did he say who he was?"

Miss Annie Bea purred like the cat who'd found the cream pitcher. "Yes, he's Sheriff Bob's grandson, Tad Johnson. He said you taught him to pay checkers and took him fishing when he was a kid. He said you used to call him 'Tadpole.'"

Jake remembered little Tadpole Johnson. He was a skinny barefooted young'un who'd followed him around and asked dozens of questions; a smart, polite little fellow who'd loved to fish. His folks moved away and Jake hadn't seen him for ten years or more, but he always knew Tadpole would amount to something one day.

Miss Annie Bea wiped the counter and watched Jake from the corner of her eye. "He stopped here to ask for directions. He said he'd forgotten the way to your house."

Jake's mouth dropped open.

We all listened while Miss Annie Bea rambled on. "He said that Little Alice invited him to have Easter with you so you'd get to know each other better. He hopes you'll take him fishing again.

If a man's face could explode from a grin, Jake's would have busted wide open that day.

TO BE CONTINUED.